Sun Dog Days

SLIM RANDLES

UNIVERSITY OF NEW MEXICO PRESS   ALBUQUERQUE

© 2006 by the University of New Mexico Press
All rights reserved. Published 2006
Printed in the United States of America
10 09 08 07 06   1 2 3 4 5 6

LIBRARY OF CONGRESS CATALOGING-IN-PUBLICATION DATA

Randles, Slim.
 Sun dog days / Slim Randles.
  p. cm.
 ISBN-13: 978-0-8263-3942-3 (alk. paper)
 ISBN-10: 0-8263-3942-5 (alk. paper)
 1. Periodical editors—Fiction. 2. Cowboys—Fiction.
 3. Male friendship—Fiction. 4. Domestic fiction. I. Title.
 PS3568.A537S86 2006
 813'.54—dc22
                                    2005027957

Design and composition: Melissa Tandysh

*For Gene and Lona Burkhart
of Sequoia-Kings Pack Trains
of Independence, California,
And for Rocky Earick, my pard . . .
If the mountains could talk about us,
they'd just laugh.*

Acknowledgments

Many thanks to Dr. Carl Austin, of the geothermal plant in the Coso Mountains, who let me refresh my memories, legally this time. For my pal and mentor, Max Evans, who broke trail for the rest of us, a hearty *muchas gracias* for reading the manuscript and for his priceless criticism. For Destiny and Tony Marquez, for their faith and friendship, and much gratitude to Jean Tierney for the copy editing and for years of love and friendship.

Slim Randles
Albuquerque, New Mexico

Dogs around the sun
cats around the moon
I'll ride that pony
'long about June

Chapter One

IT IS A CURSE, in a way, but a beautiful, seductive curse.

The horses come in the night now. They come in the night some of the time, but more often just before dawn, that time when I used to get up and stumble out of the bunkhouse into the frosty snap of a desert morning. But now it's just an early morning curse, coming when my wife is asleep next to me, and the false dawn is just a streetlight outside. It is then the horses come, pounding through my memory with the same ferocity they once had when I was in the saddle. They run, these horse ghosts, with the crazy flight of the stupid and panicked, and with all this they are still given a blessed grace and fire that most men never see in a lifetime. The wild ones still live out there, I know, but I don't. Not anymore. People say you put the wild horses away and save them for other nineteen-year-old boys. People say you move to town, marry a good woman, and go to the office every day. People say this is maturity, and maturity is a good thing.

People . . .

But people haven't been there, haven't seen the frosty breath of wild horses rise like fog on a sagebrush flat on the desert mountain ranges.

People haven't sat there, holding a big roping horse quiet, both of you with muscles clenched as you reach for that rope and build a loop, just the right-sized loop, praying the horses won't see the movement or sense your position behind the hill.

Life is comfortable now. You see, the memories don't shortchange a man enough to mask the way it really was in other ways, too. The cold mornings when the bedroll felt too nice to leave, the sudden violence when a colt slams you to the ground, the rides through the wind and the snow. Memory doesn't let you forget being broke, either, or not knowing what in the world would ever become of you. It wouldn't let you forget the times you looked at the old bunkhouse cowboys, who had nothing in their lives but a wire-patched pickup truck and an old cowdog, and wondering whether that would be you in another forty years. And it didn't let you forget the terrible loneliness of being by yourself in that bedroll and wondering if there was any woman anywhere on earth who might want to share it with you.

That was nearly twenty years ago. The woman next to me is the third to share my name in these years. The two young children in the other bedroom carry another man's name, but I am the guy who gets to take them on picnics and listen to their problems. These are gems of life more precious than diamonds.

There are children with my name, too, but they live in other places with other men. They can be found only on telephone lines and on an occasional weekend when it suits their mothers. The bitterness is mostly gone now. Left in its place is just the constant dull pain that won't quiet down. The faultfinding is over. It was my fault. All of it. It's easier that way. And it's just wait and call and be alone and daydream of sharing a home with them someday.

A man I love and admire took me to one side at a family picnic ten years ago now.

"Being a man means doing what's necessary," he'd said. "Remember that. Doing what's necessary."

So now I work for a magazine in the city and drive back and forth every day and do what's necessary. But it's not bad. There's always Jan at home, with a smile softer and more knowing than angels. And there are the kids, too, and being called "Pop," and going places on weekends.

If there's some hassle at the office, it's nothing a real High Sierra packer can't handle, even if he wears a necktie now. There are always those Friday nights when a guy can have a beer and tell stories about the mountains and the mules and the horses and men whose lives touched his and he wonders whether they believe him, but he's had two beers and doesn't give a damn.

So now sometimes I lie awake and hear Jan breathing softly and sweetly beside me and try to fight the images of those horses racing down the arroyos in wild panic. Jan is my lodestone, my center. I try to forget how it felt to have a thousand pounds of roping horse beneath me, and how it was to be part of that horse as we gained slowly on the stragglers. I try to concentrate on the next month's issue of the magazine or the little bed of irises I'm trying to grow and put in a dark corner the feel of the nylon three-eighths catch rope as it flies forward past the hammered-flat ears of my horse and flares to encircle the neck of a running mustang. I try to think of how sweet Jan looks in the mornings with her sleepy smile and forget the exhilaration of a large wild animal slamming into the end of that rope, spinning around and screaming.

Damn these hauntings! There should be an antimemory pill for ex-cowboys. You think of a horse ... hey, drop one of these babies and wait twenty seconds and the desert haze disappears and the smog and traffic return.

It would keep a man's mind on the traffic instead of looking at a sour dark cloud over Los Angeles and being taken from the center lane to the back of a gentle horse moving slowly down the darkly canyon trails as the sun kisses the faraway Inyos goodnight like a gift to a blazing whore. And then I could hear the radio news instead of the horses and mules snuffling for the *morals* full of rolled barley we hung on their heads. I'd listen to the horns honking, instead of the creaking of the packs on the mules as each slid down a piece of slickrock on the high switchbacks.

But it's too easy to recall the ribald lies that made weary cowboys laugh with eyes red from too many hours in the saddle. When I step on the gas, I can still feel the coiled-spring tension of the bronc as I ease my spurs up over the shoulders and nod for the gate. On drives home in the rain, I can almost trade the rhythm of the wipers for the hooves of my horse picking its way down the trail. The sheen on the glass lets me feel again the jet of icy water pouring off the funnel of my hat brim onto the neck of my horse as the light fails down the mountain toward the fog-shrouded lights of the pack station.

It is a disease, a lingering malady nearly invisible to others who don't have it. It is a disease that sits just below the surface, waiting for its chance to break out again and ruin a guy's carefully thought-out life. It is a disease caught by just a few. Just a few of the luckiest, most blessed people in the world.

And in these soft hours of morning, when the lacy curtains begin to take form and when the pictures of the children on the dresser still show only as silhouettes . . . in this most vulnerable of times in a man's day . . . the horses come. Those beautiful blessed damned horses that a man will never see again.

And if a guy should lose a tear or so in mourning, please look the other way. The horses would understand, but no one else would.

As I stir, an arm reaches across my chest, warm from sleep, and that sweet smile hits me, and the horses vanish like smoke from a dream fire.

"You awake already, Buck?" she says.

And I just nod and smile, and then I lie there basking in the feel of her arm across my chest and listen as her breathing becomes steady in sleep again. It's like a promotion, isn't it? Horses to this. I've been promoted, and I deserve it.

A man does what is necessary.

I should've known it was too good to last.

Chapter Two

REALITY HIT JUST INSIDE THE DOOR of the office. Grab coffee, loosen tie, here it came.

The big eight-page section? The one that went in the middle of the book? No sign of it. We were two days from shipping this issue and no sign of it. What was worse, of course, is we had cover blurbed this thing in living color with a big yellow splash just above the flag, which had to be done long before the magazine was shipped to the printer because the cover was in four color on heavy slick and was done on a Miehle press and you just had to *know* what you were going to have inside when you shipped it.

No sign of it. Nothing. No phone call. Eight pages with a cover blurb and a big yellow splash, and that yellow splash would be my ass if something didn't come through. Called the writer's house in Wyoming and his wife said he was off fishing someplace, she thought, and she didn't know if he shipped the story to us or not because he was always writing things for magazines and sending things off and who could keep track of all of it, and why didn't he want to get a real job anyway, and she thought he may be home Friday sometime, but don't count on it because you never could tell about him but I could try then, anyway, and what was my name again?

That's great. Big old splash right on the cover. Everything a man ever wanted to know about canoes. Turn to the middle of the magazine for the whole scoop.

It meant either that story came in tomorrow, and then got edited, set in type, and pasted up overnight, or it didn't come in at all, and we shipped a damn magazine with eight blank pages in the middle, or I could write the sucker myself, if I knew anything about canoes, and I didn't. Or, I could get on the horn and try to find another outdoor writer in the country or in the damn world who knew as much about canoes as this idiot in Wyoming did and ask him to write some five thousand words about canoes and ship it overnight to us, and that meant paying him about double what we'd ordinarily pay and what the hell would that do to the working budget?

And if the story from Wyoming came in tomorrow and I had already found someone else to write it, that meant paying a total of three times the usual amount for a story.

So I made some decisions that I trusted would get us out of this jackpot, Good Lord willing and the creek don't rise, and I took another half pill right after lunch, but it was not helping much. I would go for a walk, but the whole thing would fall apart if I did. The art director couldn't find a rifle line-up photo for javelina for that piece that was supposed to be sent over in galleys from the typesetters, and we had to redesign a waterfowl story twice because the photos were lousy. We had good ones in stock, but they had the hunters shooting off the page, and if they'd been shooting doubles, I'd have flopped them, but one guy had an autoloader and every hunter in the world knows they don't make that model left-handed and we'd get mail saying we don't know ducks from sour squab, and I'd be honor bound to print them, and I couldn't handle a bunch more of that.

So on top of everything else, Andrea stuck her head in my office and said, "I'm sorry to bother you, Buck. I know this is a bad time, but there's a guy on the phone who says he's ol' Smoke and he has to talk to you because it's a matter of life or death." She looked at me for a minute. "You know someone named ol' Smoke?"

Well, as a matter of fact, I did.

You need to understand that Smokey always showed up, sooner or later, even in the depths of Los Angeles. I never could figure out exactly how he found me after years went by, but he always did.

And his sense of timing was uncanny.

Get things going along smoothly for a change. Go ahead, get a little money in the bank even, and here he came, grinning on back with the high country in his voice and that let's-get-the-hell-outa-here look on his face.

And this time . . . of all the times to show up.

There was the eight-page insert, the rifle line-up and the waterfowl story, and we shipped in two days. And here came old Smokey, right in the middle of everything. I almost asked Andrea to say I was out (I had done that a bit, lately), but there were some things in life you couldn't deny and one of them was Smokey.

I could no more have her tell Smokey I was not in then I could deny my own children. Smokey was a large part of this terrible memory curse. He was along on most of those memories and a nosebag full of others. Of course, Smokey had been gathering even more of them, year after year, while mine had been left semistagnant and allowed to blur a little through the haze of time.

Those other packers, those grimy, laughing, stone-broke fools of the high country, those friends, were gone now. Most of the old ones died, all but old Grant, who seemed to hang on, cheating the calendar, season after season, and refusing to quit. The rest of the old timers were dead of smoking too long, or drinking too long, or just riding and laughing too long.

The young ones from those days had gone their ways, too. One was killed in a rice paddy on the other side of the world by someone he didn't even know. One was a doctor who hung Charlie Russell prints on the wall of his waiting room. One owned an electronics company not far from here. One sold insurance during the week and drank on weekends. One washed dishes for beer money in Lone Pine. One became a magazine editor who couldn't come up with an eight-page spread in the middle of the book after it was cover blurbed.

And then there was Smokey.

Smokey was the one who looked at it on the Seventh Day, saw it was good, or at least adequate, and stayed for the Eighth and Ninth. Of our long-ago band of Stetsoned knights, he was the only one still carrying the banner and forking the broncs.

The rest of us sometimes secretly hoped Smokey would buy a house and become a plumber or something, as this would tell us we made the right decision, and made it sooner. But he just grinned and kept on riding.

So when he called, on the day I was going the craziest, his old timing was working perfectly again.

His voice on the phone wiped out the three intervening years since his last appearance. "Buck? Say, pard, I'm in this little bar about three blocks from your office, and there's this here girl sitting on my lap and calling me Honey, but she don't believe me about the time we blew up that bear with dynamite. So get your ass down here and buy us both a beer."

"Smokey," I said, taking a deep breath, "you're a sonofabitch, you know that?"

"Sure. You're comin', ain't ya?"

"Give me twenty minutes."

And for ten of those minutes I just sat there, while the whole world whirled itself straight to hell around me, and grinned.

Chapter Three

"'BOUT DAMN TIME, BUCK. It's your turn to buy. Now I was sayin' to Honey here..."

Honey looked at me and smiled as if she was collecting cowboys this month and held Smokey's elbow with one hand and drinks with the other. She had been a very pretty girl at one time, but now she spent a little too much time with her makeup and dressed just a little too carefully. She had to be a faithful subscriber to her local public television station and undoubtedly sent five dollars each year to save a whale or chipmunk or something. Her drink was one of those with an exotic name that consisted of gin and mouthwash.

The lack of introduction and greeting wasn't unusual for Smokey. He didn't go in for backslapping or handshaking or how's-the-family. He wouldn't last fifteen minutes at a Kiwanis luncheon. It may be that he just didn't care about those things, but I believed it just never occurred to him that years had passed since we split the last beer. Would you shake hands with your brother if the two of you shared the same house?

Honey settled in a little deeper and kept playing with Smokey's ear, but damned if he didn't seem to notice, which was unusual for him. I got us a couple of beers and Honey had another fizz thing, and we both listened as Smokey talked of broncs and rockslides and bears and ropes and horses. Nobody could do the stories any better, either.

"Remember ol' Skip Price don't you? Down in Apache Creek? Told me he had one of them longhorn bulls get in with his cows one time, and that bull was so potent those cows were still having longhorn calves five years later."

"That's like ol' man Jenkins once said about them longhorns ... you remember him? Ran that piece over in Smith Valley, Nevada, and wouldn't pay for cheap beans? Well, he's been known to run a few of them longhorns, time and again ..."

"Say," said Honey, "you guys just gonna talk cowboy stuff all night or what?"

" ... and Jenkins said there wasn't but two things wrong with a longhorn ..."

Honey got up and staggered to the door. Smokey didn't even notice.

" ... one of them was, you couldn't keep them things at home, and the stockyards don't like to pay for horns."

And so it went. The talk turned maudlin, as talk is prone to do when nostalgia blends with alcohol. We were left a corner of the bar to ourselves, sitting in tuck-and-roll Naugahyde comfort, facing an army of empty beer bottles. The bartender looked at his watch and nodded to the chatter of a lone alcoholic left at the bar.

"Okay, Smoke," I said, grinning, "what's up?"

"What do you mean by that?" He grinned back.

"Why me? Why now?"

"Why Buckster, you suspicious old bastard, what you talkin' about? Can't I come down here and buy my old buddy a beer?"

"Hell," I said, "*I* bought the beer."

"Well, that's right, I guess." He grinned. "So can't a guy come down out of the hills and let his old pard buy him a beer once in a while?"

"Hell yes, he can," I said. "And I guess that's why you're here, 'cause the opera season's come and gone. I tried to keep Madame Butterfly around for you, but she hoisted her kimono and scooted."

"That's ol' Buck for you," Smokey said. "Always thinking of his pard. Why, I'll bet there just ain't much ol' Buck wouldn't do for his old pal, too."

"I knew this was comin'," I said. "What's up?"

"You sound suspicious, amigo."

"Smokey, I happen to know you're allergic to any town with more than five hundred people in it, and here you are, singing like a lark in the middle of eight million city folks. You don't do things like this for fun, or even for Madame Butterfly. What's going on?"

"Business, Buck."

Smokey leaned forward just as the bartender raised the lights as a gentle reminder. The old buddy I looked at now was the same, but a bit different, too. I could see that some of the curly hair sticking out from beneath the sweat-stained Resistol was now shot with gray. His smile, supplemented by a few more wrinkles than twenty years ago, was still the same.

"Business," he said again, trying to sound as though he read the *Wall Street Journal* every morning before graining the stock. "Big business. And listen now . . . you and me are partners, right down the line. I wouldn't consider anyone else."

"Does this have something to do with me leaving my job and my home and riding off to help a damsel in distress? Or like that time we all got drunk and decided to rope Bigfoot and sign him to a movie contract?"

"Naw," Smokey said, "that was just chicken feed stuff. Hell, Buck, a guy'd think you didn't like a little *fun*. What do you have against a little sunshine and exercise for a change?"

It must have been the beers, or maybe a twinge of guilt about being a stick-in-the-mud with my old partner, but whatever it was, it made me smile and wave him on.

"It's like this, pard," he said. "I know where we can get some horses together, and the market's right just about now. Why, people are giving five hundred dollars for a riding horse . . . just broke gentle."

"And how are we to get these ponies, he asked foolishly?" I asked, foolishly.

"Well you might ask, as they say." Smokey raised an eyebrow like he was chairman of something. "Well you might ask. This here's the best part, pard. Why, we just rope them sumbucks! Free horses! There for the taking! Right where they always been."

"Aha!" I said. "Let me guess. The Coso Mountain herd, right?"

He nodded and grinned.

"Mustangs," I said. "A bunch of broomtails. And illegal as hell."

"Well damn, Buck, they're still there and getting fatter, and nobody is even running them anymore."

"Smokey, didn't anyone ever deliver a newspaper to whichever line shack or whorehouse you been holed up in? Don't you know it's been against the law to go mustangin' for what, about seven years now?"

"Sure. Heard it on the radio. Read a piece in *Western Horseman*, too. But that don't mean it makes any sense. Heard something else, too, pard. These old ponies are getting so thick out there, having babies all over hell, a bunch of cattlemen are shooting them, and the damn government is out catching them now for kids' pets. Now if the government is catching them, why don't we? We know a sight more about mustanging than they do."

"Okay," I said. "I agree the law is stupid and we're bound to have mustangs starving to death one of these days from overpopulation. But there's another little matter you seem to have overlooked. The Coso Mountain horses live on a bombing range and it's been closed to the public since George Washington raised mules. You can't even go picnic there anymore, let alone catch wild horses."

Smokey grinned. "Cuts down on the competition, don't it?"

"Okay. Legalities aside. I've got a home now, and a good-paying job, and I can't just up and..."

"Pard," he said, shrugging his shoulders and smiling. "You've had jobs and wives before... and this is a chance for some big-time money. Why, we could catch a dozen of those babies in a week or two..."

"You know better than that."

"Okay... say a month. Say a damn *month*. What the hell? Is a month going to kill us? And there we'd be, splitting thousands of dollars for a month's work. How much you make for editorializing, anyway?"

"Steady money. Good, steady money."

"Okay. But do you *love* it? I mean, do you wake up every morning and say, 'Boy, I just can't wait to get to the office and do some write-ups and tell people a bunch of bullshit that nobody believes'?"

I laughed. "Never really thought of it that way, to be honest."

"'Course not. You're too close. Bet you like to dress up and go out to lunch and everything, don't you?"

"Well, for business sometimes..."

He grabbed my arm. "Buck... Buck... can't you see what they've done? I bought a magazine and read what you wrote last month. I did. One itty-bitty story on how wonderful a certain pair of binoculars is. Right? And another story that was five pages long... and with all the bullshit stomped out of it, it just said to hunt the high timberline for mule deer until the heavy snows drive 'em down. Right?"

"I guess you could put it that way," I said, laughing.

"No other honest way to put it, pard. You didn't think of it that way because they've got you staked out and hobbled. When was the last time you had some fun?"

"Hell, I have fun all the time. We went to a party just last Friday night and had a ball."

"Party, huh? Let's see. You wouldn't like them parties where middle-aged salesmen get drunk and flirt with their friends' wives."

He looked at me as if in evaluation. It was the look of one who has been paid well to size something up and later report to the board. He took long seconds to do it, and I was impressed by his thoroughness.

"Nope. Friends' wives are out. Ain't your style. Let me guess. You like parties where everybody is a artist, right? Some of them paint pictures nobody buys, and some write stories nobody reads because the world ain't ready for them yet, and a bunch more of them do statue things out of clay that always look like they melted before they set hard."

I laughed.

"Oh yes," Smokey said, "I damn near forgot the musicians. They're the ones that always bring their guitars, or they play them little snake charmer flutes, and they write their own music with words nobody can understand . . . but they pretend they do . . . and they all like you because ten thousand people read your stories every month."

"Two million."

"Okay, two million, then. Knothead. What's the difference? You can't even start to know half of them people, anyway. And I bet your wife is proud of you at those parties because you write two million words every month, too, right? You do have a wife, don't you?"

"Yes."

"You usually do. Now be honest for a minute, Buck. Can you honestly say them parties is fun? I mean *real* fun?"

The haze of alcohol was making my toes numb up a little by this time, so I just smiled. You should never interrupt a great artist at work.

"Hell, Buck, them city people just stay serious all the time. I've met 'em and I know. They worry about the world blowing up, and someone dumping crap in the river, and not a one of 'em is smart enough to know there ain't a single damn thing they can do about it."

Smokey grinned and sipped his beer. He paused to let the intrinsic value of what he'd just said sink in. One must be cautious before discounting philosophies conjured up by looking down at the ears of a cowhorse for many years. Proper respect should be given at all times.

"They can't do a damn thing, but they keep worrying about it, Lord. And they talk about it, too. Hell, you'd think they was the Secretary of Everything and they had to decide all this stuff by eight in the morning. Now you tell *me* those guys are fun."

I laughed. "Well, it does seem to be against the rules to laugh..."

"Aha! So the Ol' Smoker begins to make sense, does he? Well now, tell me true, when was the last time you *really* had fun?"

"You mean like your kind of fun, Smoke? Let's see... when was the last time I pinched a married waitress and invited her to go skinny dipping in the river?"

"Amen," he said, grinning.

"When was the last time I walked up to some tattooed giant on a motorcycle and told him I thought he was a pansy?"

"Now you're cooking!" he said.

"No, wait. I got it... when was the last time I got drunk and passed out while singing 'Little Joe the Wrangler'? I'm trying to remember the last time my mind could see no further than the next cold beer and hot motel room. Gee, Dr. Smokey, it's kinda hard to recall."

"Yeah, I know." He grinned. "But at least now you're trying."

I grinned and shook my head.

"Buck," he said, leaning closer, "how long you been afoot, now?"

"Too damn long, Smoke. That's the truth. Just too damn long."

"Buck, to my way of thinking, afoot are the two saddest words in the English language."

I laughed. "I give up."

"Good. Then it's a deal?"

"What's a deal?"

"The horses . . . what else?"

"The horses? Smokey . . . pard . . . let me explain this to you plainly and simply. Yes, I was a cowboy and packer when I was young. Yes, I had some real good times. And yes, sometimes I miss all of it. A lot."

Smokey sat back, resigning himself to a reluctant education, bracing himself against the coming onslaught of logic, girding his thought processes against common sense. This was usually successful, too.

"Yes," I told him. "I miss it. But somewhere along the line I went crazy and attended college. And while I was in college, I learned some really strange things, like there are some interesting things to do that don't necessarily take place on the back of a horse. There are interesting people to meet and places to go that can be reached by jet planes. There are restaurants to eat in that give you napkins made out of real cloth, and they serve meals that are even better than the cheeseburgers at the Pines Café in Independence."

I drank some more and I remember thinking beer was a pretty good thing to have around.

"There are people, Your Imperial Smokeness, who are doing things in this world, and a whole lot of them live right here in Los Angeles. And there is something damn nice about waking up in the morning and finding you're not alone in a bedroll in a sandstorm."

Smokey just shrugged.

"There's only two things wrong with that kind of life, Buck. It costs too much, and you can't do it horseback. Hey, I'm hungry. Let's get some breakfast." He looked at me and grinned. "One more thing, pard."

"What's that?"

"Who the hell's this Madame Butterfat you were going to fix me up with?"

Chapter Four

THERE WAS THAT DAMP QUIET to the air in the coffee shop parking lot when we finally came out. It was the peculiar dawn of Los Angeles, when the sun doesn't rise in the east, but the light seems to increase through the haze more by some celestial rheostat than by the turning of the earth.

Smokey stopped by the door of my pickup and rolled a slow smoke while I filled my pipe. We weren't exactly sure what came next. There would be hell to pay at the house, as I had forgotten to phone, but there really wasn't anywhere else to go either. We looked at the palm fronds hanging limply from the tops of the tall, nude trunks and listened to the cars drive by during that awkward time between headlights and no headlights.

"Sure wish you'd change your mind, Buck. It could be a hoot."

"You know how it is," I said, not wanting to meet his eyes.

"You just think I'm out after a little fun, right? Ol' Good-time Smokey off on another crazy hoot? Well, I don't blame you, Buck. Been that way a long time, right? Not this time, though, pard."

"You need the money that badly?"

"To hell with the money. It ain't the money. Believe it or not, I even have some saved in a bank account, and there are a few traveler's checks stashed away in my war bag. Must be getting old to do that, eh?"

Smokey grinned, but there was something else in his grin that muted it. Something more than just the exhaustion caused by an all-nighter, too. But maybe it was just the screwy morning light they have in L.A. that made a guy see more than what was there.

"Okay," I said, striking my third match and leaning against the dented bed of my Dodge truck, "you don't need the money and it isn't just the fun of it. I realize you can't run wild horses alone, and I'm really flattered you asked me of all the buddies you've had over the years, too. So why is it so important to drop everything and go run mustangs right now?"

"I don't suppose telling you it's real important would be good enough anymore, would it?"

I shook my head.

He threw the twisted butt of the smoke to the asphalt and stubbed it out, then looked at me. "I didn't want to tell you this, but I guess I have to. It's ... well, it's a cancer thing ... and there's nothing they can do about it."

"What?"

"It can happen to anyone, I guess." He smiled softly, and I saw clearly then the lines around the eyes that came of laughing for forty years and the true extent of the gray in the curly black hair.

"Are you sure?"

He nodded.

"Where ... where is it?"

"Well, the stomach, sorta," he said, holding his belly. "Down in here, anyway."

"Did the doctor say ... say anything about how much time ... I mean ..."

"Enough time, Buck. We have enough time for a real good one. It won't really start hurting for a while yet."

I just looked at him. There were so many things....

"Nothing to say," Smokey said, shaking his head slowly. "There's no need to say a damn thing. It's good just to see you again, Buck."

I walked across the parking lot, and then back to him. He was grinning, damn him!

"Smokey," I said, slowly and carefully. "This isn't just some bellyache you think is serious now?"

"Ever know me to bitch about a bellyache?"

I shook my head. "Dammit, Smoke!"

"Yeah, I know."

"Dammit to hell!"

"Amen to that."

"Who'd you go see, old Doc Johnson?"

He nodded.

"He's older than dirt and probably can't see. Look, you need to go to a specialist, Smoke. There's a chance it may not be too bad ... there's a chance ..."

He smiled and shook his head. "Doc sent me to the hospital. Stuck me full of holes and drained my crankcase. Took pictures. I got it all right."

I slammed my fist into the truck. "Well, look. How about you go see a doctor here, huh? A specialist? Maybe there's something those doctors up in the valley don't know about yet. Hell, they're always coming up with new stuff, right? All the time. They're working on this night and day. Listen, would you go if I took you?"

"You know I hate goin' to doctors worsen herdin' sheep."

"For me? How about just going once for me?"

"Pard," he said slowly, looking up at me from beneath his hat brim, and smiling just enough to make you want to slap hell out of him, "I smell a little horse tradin' comin' on."

"How you figure?"

"Oh, like maybe something you want for something I want."

It's strange how it is. There's this rubber gasket that seals off the door to every pickup truck in the world. If you stand in a parking lot at the break of day and stare at one long enough, you begin to notice things. Like mine had this big bug caught in it. Looked like he'd been dead a long time. His head was crammed in there between that rubber gasket and the frame of the truck. Made a guy wonder how he got there and when he got there. Did he crawl in that far and suffocate? Was he trying to fly into the truck just as I slammed the door shut? You stand there long enough and look around, you'll notice things like that bug.

I unlocked the truck, brushed the bug from the rubber gasket and got in. "Let's get out of here. Where's your gear?"

"Greyhound station."

"We'll get your gear and I'll fix you a bed in the spare room at the house."

"Thanks, Buck, but I'd better not stay with you. You know the way wives feel about me. You can just take me to a hotel someplace."

"Bullshit. The last time, well, she was one of those who never left town, you know?"

"And this one?"

"Jan's quite a woman. She'll understand. This one's a winner. Wait 'til you meet her. Hell . . ." I smiled. "She might even like you."

"Well, okay, if you think it'll be all right."

Smokey turned on the radio to country music after he figured out how to get it off the FM band, and I was just as glad he did. Let the simple problems of drinking and cheating and driving a truck come straight to me in three easy-to-finger guitar chords. Sing it, Waylon. I needed something else to think about, something to make me tap my left hand on the steering wheel. Smokey sat back enjoying a smoke with his hat cocked back in the dawn light, grinning at a sleepy Los Angeles as though we'd caught the giant monster in an embarrassing moment. Besides, it was hard to think of anything to say as we drove the empty streets to the suburbs at the base of the San Gabriel Mountains.

"I'll just wait for you here in the truck," Smokey said as we pulled up in front of the house. The lights were already on and there was smoke coming from the chimney.

"I'll just tell her you're here. I won't be a minute."

Chapter Five

"JAN," I SAID.

She was sitting, sipping coffee in the living room, and had a fire going in the fireplace. She looked lonely and very tired, sitting there in a bathrobe.

"Jan," I said again. "I'm sorry."

"Are you all right?"

I nodded.

She smiled with relief and said nothing as I moved over to sit beside her. I explained about Smokey, whom she hadn't heard of except through two-beer legend.

"And he's out in the truck?"

"Yes."

"You could have called. I was really worried."

"I know, sweetheart. I'm sorry. It was just so good to see him again I kinda lost track of the time."

She sat quietly and just watched the fire through the steam of her coffee for a few minutes. For just a second, because of the light, I could see how she would look when she got old. She would still be beautiful.

"I'd like to take him to Dr. Ramsey and get some tests done. Country doctors don't always know everything."

She looked at me and shrugged. "I know he's your friend, but I'm sure his doctor knows what he's doing."

"Probably. But if there's a chance he's wrong . . ."

"It'll cost."

"It'll cost something, yes."

"It'll cost a lot. Does he have insurance?"

"He's a cowboy."

"You don't care how much it'll cost, I guess."

I had to think about that a minute. "No, I guess I don't really care how much it'll cost. That doesn't matter right now."

"Buck, I know he's your friend . . ."

"Partner."

"Okay." She shrugged. "Your *partner* . . . but you have a family now, remember? Your family has to come first."

"Of course it does. It always will, Jan."

"Will it, Buck? What about the next partner of yours who comes to town looking for a handout? Won't it be the same then?"

"He's not looking for a handout, Honey. He's sick and needs to be with folks for a while, that's all."

"And if he stays here, pretty soon you'll be wanting to go off with him someplace, probably, to help him take care of his business."

She looked at me. She raised an eyebrow. "Well?"

"Look, Honey, this isn't the time to bring it up. I mean it's early in the morning. You're tired. I'm tired. Let me just bring him in and fix him a bunk upstairs and we can talk about it later, okay?"

"Talk about *it*? My God, there *is* something."

"Just for a couple of weeks, that's all. It's not important."

Her eyes went cold. "I've heard that before."

"Not from me, you haven't."

"It doesn't matter. I've heard this before and I know where it leads."

"No you don't," I said. "You think it leads to my being gone longer and longer on business and then you find out I'm out with a younger woman and we bought a mobile home and she's having a baby and I leave you with the kids, right?"

She put the coffee down and cried.

"I'm not Jim," I said. "Honey, on the meanest day I ever spent on this earth, I wasn't like Jim. I know we've only been married a few months, but you have to learn I'm Buck, not Jim. I don't ever do things like that. Hey." I smiled, turning her head toward me. "I'm bad enough without having Jim's faults, too."

She gently pushed my hand away and turned to face me with her legs tucked primly beneath her.

"Leave the children's father out of this."

"I'd love to, Hon, but ol' Jim just keeps living with us, doesn't he?"

"He has nothing to do with this."

"Okay," I said. "He has nothing to do with this. This is between the two of us, and that's the way I want it, too. Now, how about letting me go get ol' Smokey out of the truck before he thinks we're not friendly, and we can all get some sleep."

"Where are you going?"

"To bed, of course. I'm whipped."

"I mean with Smokey. You know what I mean."

"Oh, we're just going to chase some horses around for a couple of weeks. It'll be like a little vacation, that's all."

"Chase horses?"

"Smokey wants to go run wild horses one more time. The way we used to. Before the cancer gets too bad. You know. Once more for old time's sake. That sort of thing."

"You *are* kidding."

"Jan, he's been a cowboy all his life. Why shouldn't he want to go out and chase a horse while he still can?"

She sat quietly, this time with her face in profile to me, and it was impossible to see any expression on it. It was the face of someone who either can't think, or does nothing else. I wanted to go get a cup of coffee, but Smokey was still in the truck.

"You know, I left Smokey playing the radio out there and I'd better go get him before I end up with a dead battery, what do you say?"

She shook her head quickly.

"Jan?"

"No," she said. "I don't think that would be a real good idea just now."

"Look, I said I'm sorry for not calling, okay? You're going to love this guy. And the kids? Hey, Smokey has stories, I mean . . ."

"Smokey may have stories, but I think he'll just have to tell them to other people right now," she said, straightening her back. "You can go find him a room someplace, and Buck, if you're going to take him to a doctor, it'll have to be out of your money. I need things for my home and my children, and we can't afford to support some cowboy right now."

"I can't take him to a hotel, Jan," I said, quietly.

"And why not? You can stay out with him all night."

"Don't do this, Jan."

"Don't do what?"

"He's my pard . . . my partner. I can't take him to a hotel when we have a room here."

"He's your partner. And what am I? Just a wife? Just another of your wives? Stick around while it's fun and go find another later?"

"It's not like that. It's never been like that."

"Then why do you get married so much? Did you bring Smokey home to them, too?"

"I thought we agreed we wouldn't bring them up. It's not fair. Look, I love you. I can't do anything about being married before. I can't change that. You can't change having been married before, either. It's not fair to bring that up."

"And it's fair to stay out all night with me thinking you're dead or sick or you found a girlfriend in a bar?"

"I'd never do that."

"Wouldn't you? Well, maybe you wouldn't and maybe you would, too. I'm beginning to think I don't know very much about you. And now this Smokey comes and wants you to just drop everything and go off to chase wild horses around?"

"Jan, he's sick. If he weren't sick, hey, I promise I wouldn't even consider something like this."

"Sure."

"It's only for a few weeks. You and the kids have enough money. It's not like you'd need to have me here. And then I'll be home. Look, Honey, it's just a one-time thing."

"You go now," she said, hushed and carefully, one word at a time, "and I don't know if you should come back."

"You know you don't mean that."

"No?"

"Please don't talk like that. Please think about this."

"Like you thought about us last night?" she said, her words coming cold and straight.

Oh God, no. Please. There it was again. That chill in the voice. I was done for. Oh please, not this time, too. I could feel the tears start and I just sat there and listened to her take me apart very slowly and efficiently in her mind. When I thought she was finished, I just said, "I have to go on this."

"Then go," she said, and walked into the bathroom.

I thought, why can't she understand? It's just for a little while. It's for a partner. Just something for a partner. She has to understand. She has to. I love her and the kids and what we've started together.

Maybe we could talk in a few days. Maybe I would call her in a few days. I called the publisher at home and left a lengthy message on his answering machine, then I spent some minutes getting things together and putting them by the door.

Jan was still in the bathroom. I walked to the door and knocked softly.

"Jan? I'm sorry I hurt you. I wouldn't do that for anything. It's just..."

"Please just go," she said. I could tell she'd been crying. "Just go now. We can talk about it some other time."

So there's hope, I thought. Oh God, father in Heaven, let there be hope. I can't lose this marriage. I've failed so miserably before. I can't lose this woman. She has the love glow, the touch. She has the promise of years in her eyes, except for this morning. It can't die.

"I'll just go in and say goodbye to the kids, Honey," I said through the door.

"I think it would be better if you didn't," she said. "I'll tell my children what they have to know about this. Is there anything else?"

I guess not, Jan. I guess not. Just the whole world. The whole damn world and happiness and sweet moments. I started to say something, but wisely shut up. The smarter I got, the less I talked at times like these.

"I'll see you in a few weeks," I said. She didn't answer.

I crept in and kissed the kids while they were asleep and marveled at how beautiful sleeping children are. I wanted to wake them and tell them I loved them and Pop would be back soon, but that would have to wait.

I looked around the house, her house, actually, and wondered if it was for the last time. While I packed stuff in my war bag, I thought about what I was doing, and I didn't like it, but what the hell could I do about it? I said I was sorry. She wasn't going to miss me for a couple of weeks, and then we'd be back together.

I found my spurs and rope and gently laid them in the war bag where they wouldn't get bent, packing some socks and a Levi jacket on top. Then I changed to boots and jeans and grabbed the gray 5x beaver Resistol.

My marriage with Jan wasn't perfect, of course. No marriage is perfect. We both went into this with the brakes set pretty hard. No two people, even pards, get along perfectly.

Every couple has differences. Last year I went to counseling. Wanted to see just what the hell was wrong with me. I wondered what that counselor would say to do now, at dawn in a warm house with a good woman holed up in the bathroom and my best friend playing country music on the truck radio and reading outdoor magazines. Those counselors didn't seem to be where you needed them when you needed them.

I hadn't been much at praying for long years. I thought churches were boring, for the most part. But I had this thing to do with Smokey. He didn't have anyone else, and it was the kind of thing a guy couldn't refuse.

Hey, I thought, maybe this will prove to be one of those little differences every married couple has. Every marriage is full of them, right? Since men and women are different. And you had to expect these things and surpass them all in a manner that would send you both down through the happy golden years in a blissful state of compromise.

I'm ready for that compromise, Jan. I'm ready for the work. Give me a couple of weeks now and I'll give you years, girl. Just trust me and I'll be home . . . tell the kids I love them. Tell them . . .

Tell them. . . .

Tell them what? That Pop had to go cowboying and couldn't even wait long enough to say goodbye? Please don't say that. Let them believe in me a little. Let them realize there are some things a man just has to do.

And right then I was angry at Smokey. How dare he get cancer now? Maybe if Jan and I were married for a full year . . . maybe then. Oh hell, it wasn't his fault, of course, but *dammit!*

And he was my pard.

But I was still mad at Smokey's cancer, and the pretty lady locked in the bathroom, and that outdoor writer off fishing in Wyoming on some unknown creek, and a publisher who wouldn't even talk to a man when he called.

I got my saddle out of the closet.

"Buck?"

She was standing in the open bathroom doorway. I looked at her and then she smiled. That smile. The one that said this is why she married me. Look at this smile and see the warmth and the promise and the days in front of a fire and the secret little touchings of the hand.

I crossed to her and kissed her as she smiled. Gently, lips barely touching, and I knew it was because I didn't want to do anything wrong. I wanted this to be perfect . . . a perfect point in life.

And she took my hand and led the way into the bedroom and turned off the light and pulled down the shades so there was just a marginal hint of daylight around the edges. She smiled at me and then turned away and began to undress. She undressed slowly, and I savored each part of it and was almost unaware that I was taking my own clothes off. She stood there with her back to me, waiting to be touched, and I looked at the smoothness of her skin and I thought of the way it felt to touch it, and then I walked up and put my hands where her waist began to flare into those delicious hips and felt her tremble. And I knew this was good. This was the way things were supposed to be for us both.

Then Jan turned and took my mouth and my body and my entire senses places they'd never known before, until we were both sweating and smiling at each other in the tangle of morning sheets and a strengthening light outside. And I could just catch the hint of country music on the truck radio.

"Oh Honey," I said, kissing her. And I knew I would carry that taste with me forever.

I got up and began dressing. "Hey, I'll give you a call when I get up there and know a little more about what's going on."

"You're still going?"

I stopped dead still. "I thought . . ."

She turned her back to me on the bed and pulled the sheets up to her neck.

"Honey?"

There was no answer. And somehow I knew there wouldn't be.

I went out onto the porch with my saddle, bedroll, and war bag.

Smokey came out of the truck, grabbed the saddle, and threw it in the back. He was smart enough not to ask any questions.

I pulled the truck away from the curb a little faster than normal.

"You mind waiting 'til we get up on the Crest before we roll out and get some sleep?"

"Sounds good," he said.

"Good. Let's get the hell out of here."

Chapter Six

WHAT IS THERE TO THIS TUGGING, this anchor, this brake? Why, when this should be so right, does everything feel so wrong?

The pickup truck angled past the hillside homes, which get progressively more expensive as they climb the San Gabriel Mountains, and then the last of them are behind, and there's the national forest sign and we're in that strange combination of brush and stickers and vertical rocks and manzanita that makes up the chaparral country of California and makes it the most dangerous place to fight forest fires ... anywhere.

And before when I drove this direction, up the hill, away from the city, it was like a never-ending liberation. Behind me down the hill were boyhood, school, smog, and an image of me that I didn't like. And as I climbed higher, this had always been a going forward to something better.

But this time there was a dragging, a reluctance. Behind me now, down the hill now, in that little white house now, were three people I loved. And the little arms of the children tugged at me to come back, and the smile of that sweet woman ... that morning smile, the one that started my day right, every day, was keeping me from pushing down harder on the gas. As I climbed up the rocky, scrubby canyon, the visibility grew, and below was the basin full of smog, sitting like a choking monster on the lives and lungs of millions. But I didn't want to leave it this time. I wanted the love, but not the city. I wanted the smiles in the mornings, I wanted the laughter of the children when I told them stories, I wanted to feel the warm, sweet breath of that woman sleeping beside me. I didn't care that it was her home. That was the price I had to pay. OK, so it wasn't my place. She said it didn't bother her and that her things were there. Yes, it bothered me for a time. I didn't get to put the roof over our heads, and I wanted that. Something very basic in me wanted to do that.

But that was a price I agreed to and learned to live with. She teased me about civilizing a cowboy, and she did that by a dozen little things around the house, little rules. A dozen, maybe a hundred. But that was the price I agreed to and learned to live with. Because she was truly worth it. Without the kids, she would still be worth it. If we lived in a tent, she would still be worth it. She believed in me. She believed in my writing. She believed I'd do well in it someday. Maybe she was right. I just fervently wished, right now, that she wanted Smokey to come in and sleep in that guest room.

I wished she could see this trip from my point of view. I wished that, just for an hour, she'd been a cowboy and could understand the code. The code ... rather The Code ... the same code used by our ancestors when they swam the huge Texas herds across dangerous rivers. In those days, the men paired off to swim the cows across the swollen rivers to safety on the other side. There were about a dozen things that could happen while crossing a river, and only one ... swimming the horse safely across ... was good.

Their choice of partner on that most dangerous of jobs was critical. You picked someone you could absolutely trust with your life, because that's about what it came down to.

Since those days just after the Civil War, the highest compliment one cowboy can give another is still simply, "He'll do to swim the river with."

And the code ... The Code ... says your partner comes first, and if there's something that must be done, it simply must be done.

But that didn't stop the terrible aching in the pit of my stomach as the pickup truck strained at the bonds of love and the memories of tears with each switchback up this mountain. That didn't stop me wondering whether I was a cowboy or a magazine editor, a husband or a partner, a loyal friend or a deserter.

Both. Please, both. Let there be room in life, in the universe, for both, because I can't decide this alone, I have to know what is right. All I want to do is what is right, but I don't want to ever lose that warm arm across my chest in the early mornings.

I want that smile for my warmth, my anchor, my reason for being. I want it all. All of it. God help me. I'm an undeserving selfish bastard, but I want it all.

But the pickup just kept making switchbacks and taking me farther away from the smile and picking up speed on the straightaways and I hated myself for it.

We stopped on the Angeles Crest at the first things that looked like pine trees and rolled out our bedrolls in the warm sunshine. And in that soft time between the relaxing of the muscles and the mesmerizing hum of the occasional car on the highway, I remembered only the hurt on that beautiful woman's face down below there in the haze. The hurt that I had never wanted to put there. I'd been caught before in the scissors kill-grip of decision between what I should do and what I had to do. And now it had happened again.

But this time, it would work. This time, it had to work. Because I remembered other things, too . . . things that tipped the scales in favor of things working out.

☀

She was the prettiest woman at the meeting that night, that gathering of writers and artists and others with some political ax to grind, and I had to go because they told me to, wanted me to write a piece about it for the magazine, boss's pet project. So I went, but I kept seeing her there, and I swear I wouldn't have done anything myself. I was a divorced man and had no right—in my mind—to think about the possibility of being happy again.

"You've met Jan, haven't you?" my boss asked.

"What?" I turned around and she was standing next to him.

"Jan, this is Buck."

"Hello . . ." she said, and she smiled and I was finished.

There are smiles you only dream about in the lonely hours, and this was one of them. This was the smile. The girl who has haunted my dreams since I was maybe ten? The dream girl? She has that smile, too. The perfection. The smile that says, "I like you anyway, no matter what, and I find things about you that make me happy, and I'm on your side. See how I smile at you in your dreams? That's the way it will be in real life someday when you find me. I'll be there. You'll find me."

The dream girl was a dark brunette, because dream girls have to be something, and Jan was a blonde, but I didn't care, because the smile was there. The same smile. I was done and didn't know it.

So I chatted politely, and she wanted to know about my work, and I asked about her job in the art gallery, and I pretended to be interested in artists who didn't make any sense. But I thought this time, this happy, special time, was a one-time thing. For now, the smile was on me. Maybe just this time, but it was there and it was for me. I was sure glad I came.

But I didn't ask for her number. I wanted to, but I didn't think I'd enjoy being rejected again, so I let it pass. We went back to our lives.

For two days. Then my phone rang at the office. It was Jan. Did I remember her? Yes, of course, how are you? Just fine, she said, but I have a problem. What problem? There's a loose step on my stairs going up to the attic, and I wondered if you could help me fix it. Well, see, Jan, I'd love to, but there's a million other people better than I am with a hammer, and I'm just not good at all that way.

Well, you'd be doing me a favor if you just came over and looked at it and gave me some advice; would you be willing to do that? And if you have the time, you could have some dinner with us. I'm sure the kids would like to meet a real cowboy.

Sure. That would be fine. Where do you live?

I went over and maybe I looked at the step and maybe I didn't. I don't remember. But dinner was delightful, and the kids were fun, and later we sat by a fire in the living room and I told some stories before bedtime, and the kids hugged me goodnight and that was kinda wonderful.

Then Jan came back and we each had a glass of wine and stared at the fire and talked about our exes and our plans, and I discovered I really didn't know what my plans were. And I discovered something else, too. This had nothing to do with a loose step. This happened because she was interested in me.

She gave me a little hug at the door as I left that evening, and I knew I wanted more.

The evenings multiplied, the hugs grew more intense, the hugs changed to kisses and then to passion and the evenings lasted until breakfast, and after a few months, we were married.

☀

"You got trouble at home?" Smokey asked.

"Nothing I can't handle."

But maybe that wasn't the truth. Maybe this would prove to be just too much for two people to handle. Whatever came of it, I had a job to do now, and I was going to do my best to put it on the back burner for a few days and concentrate right now on just being Smokey's pard.

And then the breeze through the pine needles and the soft scent of the duff beneath my bed tarp mingled with the pungent odor of the sweatband on my hat, pulled down over my nose. The mixture took me back about twenty-five years to the ranch and the sharp tangy snap of the alkali and the dust rising up and coating sweaty armpits on Western shirts as the horses and mules milled about in the corrals out at Blackrock.

"What do I do?" I asked Ross that day.

"Shoe mules, kid," he said, looking at me strangely. "What else are you supposed to do when you come out here and see five men shoeing a hundred head of mules? I mean, Jesus Christ . . ."

"I've never done that."

"What?"

"Shoe mules. I've never learned to shoe."

Ross looked at me as if I'd just crawled out from under a rock and, not taking his eyes off me, yelled to a young packer bent over a hoof, "Smokey! Show this gunsil how to shoe."

To my surprise, Smokey wasn't any older than me. But I knew he'd been there. You could see it. He straightened up slowly, grabbing the small of his back and stretching up through a grimace.

"What's your name?"

"Buck."

"Buck, don't be stupid. Don't learn to shoe. Don't ever learn to shoe. Tell Ross you got a bad back or something. Jeez, a man's gotta be crazy to shoe."

"I want to be the best mule shoer in the High Sierra," I told him.

Smokey walked completely around me, and it made me nervous for a time there as he looked me up and down.

"Buck, old son," he said, "I'm just damn near seventeen years of age, and in all my time I never heard nothing so stupid. You see, when you learn to put shoes on a horse or mule, and you don't come down with the galloping spinal taps or pee-waddles of the pelvis, then you'll get stuck with every damn head of killer stock in the country. Won't nobody look at you like you was smart . . . ever again. And you think, well hell, it's only for three months a year we gotta put iron on these bastards and then we got all winter long to rest up and drive to town and terrorize women. Just ain't the way it works."

This was the first inkling I had of my new partner's role in the world of philosophy. Smokey stretched again and walked to the shade of a giant locust tree. He looked around for a blade of the tough salt grass that was just right, then kind of shuffled his feet, stuck the grass between his teeth, and collapsed into a proper hunker.

I grabbed the first glass blade I found and hunkered next to him. Smokey picked up a good stout twig and began drawing in the white powdery dust.

"The worst of it," he said, "is the girls. Buck, it's my duty to tell you this, 'cause I know you're just a pilgrim and don't know better. You think learning to shoe makes you a better packer, a better cowboy. Well, what it does is it ruins you with the girls.

"You see, girls really like horses. Don't know why unless they like being around something dumber'n they are. Which may be why we're out here, too. Well, they like those damn horses, but not just any horses. They like *spirited* horses. Got to be spirited. Now Buck, you and me we're grown up men and we both know that spirited really means meaner'n hell.

"To them, ain't nothing better than sitting on top of some anti-social, snot-blowin' killer that tries to gimp up everything in the county. All is forgiven, you see, if the bastard just prances a lot and snorts now and again. She may not be able to control him, and he might be ugly as swamp scum, but to her, he's a winner if he'll just spray bronc snot over about two and three-quarters acres now and then.

"When these girls turn about nineteen, they get rid of the horse and find a football player who's learning to sell insurance, but until then . . . Whee! They can be trouble. They'll drive you crazy, Buck. They'll come up and say, 'Buck, you're so big and strong and such a he-man packer from the high-ups, would you put some shoes on Twinky for me? If you do, then me and you could go riding out along the aqueduct and act silly and play slap-and-tickle.'

"So, like a fool, you get iron on Twinky for her. But she stands right there the whole time, so you can't just give him an Irish anesthetic or hogtie him like you should, so by the time you've clinched the last nail, you're so stoved up you couldn't do nothing anyway. Marilyn Monroe'd be safe from you if you was both in the same bedroll at Woods Lake."

Several men were cursing as they caught new mules to shoe, and Ross yelled, "Smokey, are you teaching Buck to shoe?"

"All the important stuff, Ross. All the important stuff."

Then we stood and stretched and Smokey said, "You still want to learn?"

"More than ever, Smokey."

He stuck out his hand and we shook. "Well then, hell, pard, I guess we better go catch you a gentle horse and get you started."

☼

I was stiff and hurt like hell that night, but I'd put shoes on two gentle horses and they'd passed inspection, and I hadn't quicked either one of them. I was ready to shoe mules and the world looked great.

Smokey grinned at me as we splashed water over most of the exposed parts of our bodies and got ready to eat. How could he understand? How could he know what it meant to be living at long last like Zane Grey and Will James? He'd never heard of either of them, I discovered.

"Okay," he said to me as we wiped off on gunnysacks. "I want to know why."

"Why?"

"Why you want to learn to eat dirt and be sore and work out here where nobody can afford nothing."

"Smokey," I said, pointing toward the peaks that always seemed to rise straight up at dusk when the sun's rays shoot between the highest of the pinnacles, "it's about the grandest thing a man can do."

Smokey's mouth dropped open. "Dear Aunt Tillie's sainted hairnet!" he said. "I think he means it!"

☼

Weeks later, I rode bent over in the saddle as my horse picked his way up through the slickrock chute just under the very top of Glen Pass in Kings Canyon National Park. Smokey had four mules up front, there were six dudes between us, and I had three mules and brought up the caboose. The rain slashed down at us and we had to hold real still. If we moved our heads, the small lakes that formed on our hat brims spilled a river down our shirts.

Smokey stopped his string on the level area at the very top of the pass and hobbled his horse. Lightning was blasting here and there around us. I hobbled my horse, tied the lead rope of my lead mule to the horn, and walked up through the dudes to where Smokey was. He looked like a drowned rat that had just been told he was too dry.

"Damn roan mule threw a hind shoe," Smokey said.

I looked down one side of the razor-edged ridge and could just make out the outlines of Rae Lakes to the north. On the south side of the pass, the swirling rain hid the emerald and aquamarine ponds I knew were about eight hundred feet straight down from us. I also knew there were horse and mule bones there and that this wasn't a good place to even slow down during a thunderstorm, let alone stop to shoe mules. And you'd only fall off that pass once.

"You going to replace that shoe now?"

"Hell yes. Got to. You take a barefoot mule down this rock pile and before you got to Rae Lakes you'd have a crippled mule that couldn't work another day this season."

Smokey got a foot rope ready for the big flighty roan, then fished his shoeing kit out of a pack.

"You folks might as well take it easy and get comfortable," I told the dudes. "We have to put a shoe on a mule now."

"I like that *we* stuff," Smokey mumbled.

While I was loosening cinches and dudes were trying to find dry rocks, which didn't exist, one woman walked up behind the roan mule.

"We can't stop here, young man," she said. "It's raining and I'm wet and I'm cold and I'm uncomfortable and there isn't even any tree to get under and you can just wait with your chores until we get . . ."

"Shut up, ma'am," Smokey said.

"You can't speak to me like that!"

"Ma'am, just shut *up*!" Smokey said, looking around furtively and then whispering to her. "Talkin' draws lightning!"

The woman looked around suddenly and seemed to hear the crashing of the thunder for the first time. Then she sat down on a rock next to her husband.

"I'll be damned," said Smokey, grinning. "It worked. Hand me some nails, will you?"

And when he finally straightened up and put his hammer and rasp away in the shoeing kit, he looked at me through the rain and grinned.

"I guess it's about the grandest thing a man can do, right Buck?"

We'd come down for the rodeo in Bishop, too, that first season. We'd had our shot at the rough stock and Smokey bucked off a saddle bronc named Popper. First he was there, spurs singing, then he was doing a Manhattan spin over the horse's head. Popper missed stepping on him as he went over the top, grunting and bellering to the world. And the audience clapped anyway for Smokey the game kid. He'd looked awfully good while he was up there, after all.

Later we went out and had some beers down by the river outside of town because we weren't old enough to go into a bar, and Smokey couldn't get that horse out of his thoughts.

"I took too short a rein," he said. "If I'd just backed off an inch or two I'd had him rode. I mean, I had that old sumbitch dead to rights. You see how he came out and ducked back to the left? Hell, that was no sweat. I had him ridden good, but I took too short a rein. How's a guy supposed to know where to take a rein if he's never drawed a horse before? I couldn't even find anybody'd had him before."

"Hell," I said, "forget it and have a beer. I got bucked off, too. No big deal. Lots of ground. Can't hardly miss it."

"Now that's the kind of talk that'll turn you into a loser, sure as hell," he said. He finally took a pull at a beer. He looked over at me, and I knew he was serious. "You don't see what happened, do you?"

"Sure. A horse named Popper bucked you off."

"No. That's just what I mean. No. Now he's a good bronc, I'll give him that. A man could win money on that horse." Smokey reached over and slapped me on the shoulder. "You're a good kind of pard, Buck, so I can tell you this," he said seriously. "I flat bucked off that horse!"

"Hell yes you did. I saw it."

"No . . . by God no, you didn't see it like that. What you saw . . . you saw the horse buck me off. I'm telling you *I* bucked off. *I* did it . . . or rather didn't do it. I've been bucked off by good horses before. Will again. But that sucker didn't buck me off. I had him rode, but I took too short a rein and I bucked off him."

"What's the difference, Smoke?"

"Biggest difference in the world. Drink up. I'm going to go ride that wolfy ol' sumbuck tonight."

"Tonight? In the dark?"

"Why not? We can sneak over there and run him in the chute and I'll scratch some hair off that rank ol' . . ."

"That's just nuts."

"Why?"

"Well, besides there probably being some damned local ordinance against riding someone else's bronc by moonlight, and besides you taking a hell of a chance on being killed . . . why you'd be cheating him."

"What the hell do you mean, *cheating* him?"

"What if he's a crowd bucker, Smoke? Huh? What if he only does his best with about four thousand people screaming? Besides, you know damn well a horse doesn't want to buck after dark 'cause he can't see his footing. You'd go out there tonight and take the proper rein and probably ride him, but I'll bet you five bucks he won't buck as hard as he does during a regular contest ride."

Smokey was quiet for several minutes and we listened to the quiet river sucking happily at the roots of the big cottonwoods.

"You're right, dammit," he finally said. "I know you're right."

We listened to the river some more.

"Maybe you'll draw him next year," I said.

"Next year he'll be older. Maybe he won't buck as hard. Hell, maybe he'll be dead, and I'll never know. Look, I can ride that horse *now*."

The next morning, Smokey drew his pay and headed off to Tonopah, where the same string of bucking stock was to be used. He kept after it for three months before he finally drew Popper again. Out in Elko, if I'm not mistaken. Won second on him. Then he came back to the ranch for winter.

I remember thinking that sure was foolish at the time, but lying there in a sleeping bag just listening to the bugs and the trucks under what passes for a San Gabriel Mountains pine tree, I wasn't sure what I believed anymore. Too many things were changing. There were too many new things to think about.

I tried to think of anything except that here I was, alone in a bedroll again. It was very hard to push that from my mind.

And I knew it was just the start.

Chapter Seven

"I THOUGHT I HEARD YOU boys pull in this morning."

Ross smiled over his coffee cup in the low-ceilinged kitchen of the worn ranch house on the edge of town.

"Hi Ross," I said, and headed for the coffeepot.

"Thought you boys had more sense than to come back up to this starve-to-death country."

"Wild horses couldn't keep us away," I mumbled. The joke was lost on Smokey, who began telling Ross of the wild horses in our future and all the money there was to be made. I poured him a cup and remembered the sugar.

I smiled as the coffee burned away some of the fatigue of the last two days. This was home. Not the only home for me, but definitely one of them. As Ross sat quietly listening, and as Smokey warmed up his sales pitch on wild horse hunting, I looked around and wondered what made a place home. Memories, I guess. Memories of a comfort that can only come after a long tiredness.

I looked at the fly-specked flour sack curtains over the sink, hanging from the same rod that was never fixed quite right. Even the oilcloth on the kitchen table seemed to have the same worn spots, and gunnysack curtains still hid the pots and pans on the jury-rigged shelves beneath the old sink. The ceiling beam held the brands of the outfit, as did the kitchen cupboards. We'd burned those brands onto many cattle, horses, mules, and burros, and we'd proudly ridden for the outfit. The brands were a part of a home, too, and part of a heritage, like a coat of arms.

The house had always smelled of coffee, dogs, tobacco, neatsfoot oil, leather, horse manure, and saddle soap. The smells were never overwhelming unless it rained and the dogs got wet. This was a using kind of home, a home for a single man who carefully washed his dishes, but didn't always sweep the floor.

"Where's ol' Grant?" I asked when a break offered itself.

"Irrigating," Ross said and was then swept back into the conversation with Smokey over the glories of mustanging. I could remember when Old Grant was merely an old man and not quite a history lesson. Grant was related to some famous old bank robbers, but he always rode the straight trail. As a kid, he had known Butch Cassidy and the rest of the Wild Bunch up in Montana. As a young man, he rode several famous bucking horses in early contest rides and even knew Charlie Russell. Old Grant made himself a packing legend one year, probably before powered flight, by packing a full-grown grand piano ten miles through the mountains to a hunting lodge.

"Boys," he said, "it taken us ten days to clear a trail wide enough for that pianner, and when we got 'er there, we'd made 'em a road they could drive a truck in. And hell, goddang I mean to say, the way it was, now you take in there that pianner? Still in tune when we got there."

It had taken knowing the old man twenty years to get this much out of him, and we always speculated that if he lived another twenty years, we'd discover he'd been in the Civil War or discovered fire or something. And these stories were always true, too.

The very first time I met Grant, I had been looking for something to do around the ranch, and Ross said he figured I could go help Grant irrigate the alfalfa. So when Grant pulled on his rubber boots and walked out through the screen porch, I pulled on another pair and followed. He stopped in the ranch yard, looked at my boots, then slowly worked his way up my skinny frame to my young face.

"Where *you* goin'?"

"Gonna help you irrigate, Grant."

He looked at me and kinda turned his head sideways. "You been to *college*, ain't ya?"

"Yes sir. Two years now at agriculture school."

"Well hell, goddang I mean to say, the way it was, now you take in there them college boys? Ain't no college boy goin' to mess with my alfalfa," he said and just marched off. That ended that.

As I sat there in the kitchen that morning, so many years later, a thought occurred to me; we had probably broken every convention known to civilization in the last half-dozen hours. We had showed up back at the ranch after an absence of years without even calling Ross first. We had driven into his yard in the middle of the night, moved into his bunkhouse, and now walked into his house and helped ourselves to coffee without even a word, let alone a knock on the door.

In a minute, we knew, Ross would get up and start frying eggs for us that were always cooked hard with splashed grease and smothered in black pepper. I also knew I was the only one here who saw anything unusual in what we'd done, and that wouldn't have occurred to me if I hadn't spent the last few years in the city. After all, we had staked out this ranch as our home many years before, so why knock?

Ross got up and broke eggs into the cast-iron skillet.

"You know, it's an amazing thing," he said. "You take two high school boys that are short on smart but hell on energy. One of them can sit a horse okay, but doesn't know how to handle people. The other doesn't even know where the radiator is on a wheel tractor and can't milk a goat.

"Over a few seasons, you watch the one turn into a top hand who can work on any ranch or pack station in the country. The other one gets his mules in and out of the mountains okay and then comes down with a dose of smart and goes off to college. So today you have one top hand and one magazine writer, and what do they do? They chuck it all to come back up here where nobody can put a down payment on a free lunch, and they want to run wild horses, which aren't worth the time it takes to brand them. I don't know," he said, looking at us and grinning. "I hope to hell whatever brain fever you boys caught ain't catching."

"Hell fire, Ross," Smokey said, "a man's got to go run broomtails every now and then, you know."

"You get fired from that ramrod job, Smokey?"

"Hell no."

"How about you, Buck? Someone tie a can to your tail at that magazine?"

"Not yet, anyway, Ross. I got some time off coming, anyhow."

"Well, it still don't make sense."

It was hard to know just how to break it to him. While I hesitated, Ross splashed bacon grease vigorously over the eggs and reached for more pepper.

"You see, Ross," I began, "it's Smokey . . . Smokey . . ."

"Ol' Smokey said it was time for a vacation, right Buck?"

Smokey got up to head for the coffeepot and shook his head quickly in my direction.

"A real toot of a vacation. Why Ross, you shoulda seen what they had Buck doin' Down Below . . . writing stories . . . chasing secretaries . . . watching football games on television. Plumb pitiful, it was. You'd a broke down and sniffled, it was so bad. So here we are, two hands that figure to make a bundle off them Coso horses."

"You boys pretty fast?"

Ross slid the eggs onto our plates and handed us the pepper shaker in case there might be a place he'd missed. There wasn't.

"How's that?"

"Fast," he said. "You know . . . *fleet of foot*? I figured you boys would have to be pretty fast to catch wild horses afoot. I checked my corrals this morning and didn't notice any new horses out there, and I saw the saddles in the pickup. Looks to me like you boys was planning to ride something."

"Oh yeah, Ross," Smokey said quickly, "I was just about to mention that . . ."

"I thought maybe."

"You see, my pard and me figured you'd probably want in on the deal, and we both know how busy you are here with the cattle and all, so we thought, for a cut of the profits, of course, you might let us borrow Brownie and Cotton for a couple of weeks."

"Well," Ross said, "I guess you could, if Brownie was still alive, which he isn't, and if Cotton wasn't so damn old he has to have help chewing his grain."

"Sorry to hear about Brownie," I said. And I was. He'd been a good horse.

"He was at least twenty-five," Ross said. "Unlike some packers I know, horses seem to have sense enough to get old when they're supposed to. Well, I guess maybe there's a couple of ponies out in pasture dumb enough to go along and get some exercise for a while.

I won't need them until I start the gather in May. You boys have a horse trailer?"

"Well..." Smokey said.

"Well?" Ross grinned and kinda squinted his eyes and raised his eyebrows at us. He was like a lawyer... always knew the answer to a question before he asked it.

"Well, see, that's another thing, Ross," Smokey said. "We thought ... I mean now for a cut of the take and all ... that if you didn't really need the stock truck for a few weeks, and if we took care of it..."

"You boys got enough money to put gas in it?"

"Sure, Ross," Smokey said, grinning. "High test, if you want it."

"Well, I guess it wouldn't hurt."

"You won't be sorry, Ross, really. Why, we'll come back with so many horses..."

"Just make damn sure you come back with *my* horses and that stock truck."

We promised, and then I noticed the twinkle in Ross's eyes and knew it was all right.

Later that morning, we sat on the top rail of the catch pen while the horses milled around, raising the alkali dust into a twisting, choking cloud that rose over the ranch like a flag.

Ross picked out two horses for us. Mine was a tall bay with a short back and a kind eye named Chuckles. Smokey's was a fleabite roan—what we call a sabino in this country—named Duster. Those geldings looked as if they had enough bottom to pave the Pacific and sand enough in their craws to make its beaches. It turned out they had. These two geldings were out of mares roped out of the Cosos long ago and had been sired by Ross's quarter horse stud. They'd do.

We caught old Cotton out of the herd and trimmed his hooves for fun. Gave him a bait of grain, too, and it was a pleasure to hang the *moral* over his ears once again. Then we turned him out and put shoes on Chuckles and Duster and gave them some grain before putting them in the overnight pen.

The rest of the day was taken up with buying grub and getting our gear adjusted to the two horses. We borrowed their bridles from Ross's tack room, and limbered up with our ropes while Ross changed the oil in the truck.

Old Grant came in from his small cabin for dinner that evening as the spring wind made lonesome tunes through the tall locust trees around the ranch house.

He stopped just inside the door.

"I know you boys," Grant said, looking at each of us closely with his good eye.

"Smokey and Buck, Grant," Ross said.

"Smokey and Buck . . . sure," Grant said, shaking hands. Cancer had taken one of his eyes long ago, and his patch made him look like a somewhat bowlegged pirate. His clothes hung loosely on his frame, as did his face, and his felt hat had a few more grease stains. It was the same felt hat he had always worn, and we'd sometimes speculate on what color it had been originally. We could never recall having seen Grant's hair. He might have been bald.

"I heard you boys had jobs," Grant said.

"They're going to run wild horses down in the Cosos," Ross said.

Grant smiled as he sat and waited for dinner. "There's some horses in there, boys," he said, as we waited for the inevitable preamble. Here it came. "Well, hell, goddang I mean to say, the way it was . . . now you take in there them Coso horses? Plenty of bottom in 'em. Hard to get a rope on those boogers. Run plenty of good horses down trying. Got to be smart to catch 'em."

We ate in silence, each with his own memories and hopes. When we finished, we washed up and went into the small living room. Ross built a fire and we smoked.

"You boys know where the falls are?" Grant asked.

We did. The falls had only a trickle of water in them, and only fell about six feet, but they made a pretty good pool at the bottom and there was even a palm tree there. Stunted little palm tree, but it was kinda cute. Below the pool, the thirsty desert drank up the water. It was a special place.

We grinned again at the preamble.

"Well hell, goddang I mean to say, the way it was, now you take in there them Coso horses? They like them falls. Use 'em regular. But a man might better check that little seep over in Black Canyon, too, and maybe the pool at Cow Springs. You know the pool?"

We did.

"They might be working all three springs, wet as it's been. Go with you for a whistle up a whore's skirt, too."

"You know you're welcome, Grant," I said, hoping he wouldn't accept.

He chuckled. "Too old. Too goddanged old, boys." He thought a minute. "How old am I, Ross?"

"I think you're ninety-two, Grant," Ross said.

He shook his head as he rolled another smoke. "God that's old. But we've caught a few horses out of the Cosos before, ain't we Ross?"

"Quite a few, Grant."

Grant lit his thin smoke and rose to leave, but stopped at the kitchen doorway and turned back to us.

"You know, boys," he said, "there is a sorrel mare what runs with that big bunch in there. Good stuff. Clean legs. And run? She stays just behind that old lead mare. The dun. I've tried a few times to get a loop on her, but just never got up there. God that's a horse! I thought, maybe if you boys get up on her . . ."

"If we catch that mare," Smokey said, "we'll bring her back for you."

Grant smoked. "Would you do that, boys? She's got a pretty little head with a blaze face and a white stocking on her off hind leg. Can't miss her."

Grant went off to bed, and we got ready to go, too.

"You boys do me a favor, will you?" Ross asked.

"Sure," I said, "anything."

"You grab two of them fishing rods on the screen porch on your way out and put them in the truck."

"Ross," Smokey said, "there ain't enough water in the Cosos to fish in."

"Hell no. But when you guys get caught running wild horses, which is illegal, and in the Coso Mountains, which is a Navy bombing range, and you've got two horses wearing my brand and you're driving my stock truck, I aim to tell them you said you were going after catfish down in the aqueduct."

We promised to take the rods.

"You know," Smokey said, "I'm going to keep an eye out for that sorrel mare of Grant's. I'll get a rope on her, too, if I can."

Ross smiled. "You boys know that mare's probably been dead thirty years, don't you?"

Chapter Eight

THERE'S A SAYING IN THE HIGH COUNTRY that tough country builds tough horses, and I guess it's true enough.

It would be difficult to find more inhospitable country for living things than the Coso Mountains of eastern California. They take up a part of the map that no one seems to need much, and nothing was ever found there that man couldn't get more easily somewhere else.

The Cosos are not high, have no streams, no valuable minerals except in the extreme north, and any trees are a miraculous afterthought. This is a desert range. And, as if to put a cherry on the whole proposition, the mountains were completed in several fits of rude violence.

Coso Peak destroyed itself several times, belching massive amounts of lava across its desert slopes, destroying and scorching the already fragile landscape until the small range was a mass of black escarpments, fields of man-killing lava, and deathly quiet canyons going nowhere that never give up their secrets.

Even Death Valley, its more famous neighbor to the east, has more to offer man.

Horses didn't always live in the Coso Mountains. Just as man found nothing there to cherish, neither did the mustang for several hundred years. His home had been made along the Owens River in the valley full of salt grass and shade trees until the ranchers came. Then the wild horse moved into the more desolate and unwatered Saline and Panamint Valleys until the miners came along and he had to strike out once again for a new home. When even the sun-slashed Argus Range became pocked with mine shafts, the horses drew back into the one place man didn't want: the Coso Mountains.

There is one place in the mountains where the water gushes up from its hell bright hot and flows into rocky, stinking pools in the brushy flats of the main range. When cars were square and slow, a few people had come there and built buildings of stone. And other people drove a long way to get there and paid money to sleep in the stone buildings and to soak in the searing waters, hoping to boil the syphilis spirochete out of their bodies. It was the only known treatment at that time, and sometimes it worked.

When the people came, the mustangs pulled back up in the eastern ridges and watched and waited. There were other places in the mountains with water that was cold and good and they went there. There was nowhere else to go. This was their last stand.

Finally the buildings were left open to the wind and the lizards and a fence was built across the dirt road far down toward the valley where it starts to climb, and signs were put on the fence to warn people this was a Navy bombing range.

Once the man smell was gone, the mountains were all theirs once more. They learned, when the first of the horses died, that airplanes were bad, and they taught the foals to run from the noise. But they didn't leave the mountains. The screaming planes had strangely given them back this mountain range, and they learned to live with the planes as they learned to live with the mountain lions.

Wild horses have always been tough. Even in the days when the salt grass valleys were dotted with their number, there were the Paiutes to worry about, and the wolf and mountain lion. Especially the mountain lion. He would rather eat horse meat than any other delicacy on earth, and he stayed fat on the valley horses in those early days.

Then the cattle came and the horses were shot, caught, or evicted because they ate grass. The lions turned to cattle, which were much less of a challenge to catch and kill, until the rifles and dogs brought them down. Like the horse he fed on, the lion moved to the unmanned country and became as tough and wary as his prey once again.

And so it is that now only the smartest and toughest of both horse and cat live in the Coso Mountains.

The several thousand survivors of the giant herds that once roamed the salt grass now chew on the sparse dried grasses of the slopes and find summer shade in the cool dark spots beneath the lava cliffs. They come to water warily, and only in the early morning and evening, with nostrils flared like radar for that pungent odor of sour cat box that tells them they are not alone at the waterhole. If the smell is there, the lead mare will find it first, and she will wheel and trot the herd perhaps twenty miles to the next seep for an undisturbed drink.

The hooves of these horses never get long, worn short as they are by the constant rasping of the lava. Their ancestors from the cottonwood shade and salt grass days along the Owens River couldn't live here in the Cosos now. The generations of survivors have seen a gradual transformation of their hooves from the splayed amber of the sand and meadow horses to the solid black iron-hard hooves of today's Coso mustangs. It is said you can do anything to those hooves except nail on a shoe. It is tough to do so.

The Paiutes of the Owens Valley sometimes talk of the great walks they used to make across the High Sierra each summer, taking salt to the San Joaquin Valley to trade with the Lizard Eaters for potatoes. The horses they shared their valley with then were often sprinkled with light colors and patches and spots. But the Coso herd now must live amidst the bluish tinge of the sage, the mottled black of the lava, and the sandy tan of the hillsides. Today's mountain horse comes only in solid colors, ranging from light dun to black. Spotted horses are too easy to see.

Coyotes seldom go far up the rugged slopes of the Cosos, deer prefer the well-watered eastern slope of the Sierra just a few miles away to the west, and the wild burros stay around the lower fringes of the mountains, preferring the creosote bush and sage of the lower country.

The high-up rough stuff of the Cosos is left pretty much to the eagle, the lion, the mustang, and to a very few men who trespass to find them.

Chapter Nine

THE HEADLIGHTS BORED HOLES in the black desert morning. In the back, the jostling of the horses made comfortable rocking motions for Smokey and me up in the cab. Our bellies were full of breakfast from the all-night café in Lone Pine, and we were headed for the tules.

As I took the turnoff to Death Valley and began to skirt dry Owens Lake, I marveled at how this country never leaves a man completely. There was something there that spelled strength and hope and fun even when it may be hard to find.

Even then, in the predawn hours of an early spring day, there was a part of it that followed a man. It may be the combined smell of the alkali and salt grass. Like sourdough starter, it left a crisp, sharp scent very much like wet soap after a shower, and mixed with it is that tinge of sharpness and hardship that all desert dwellers come to know. After one of the few priceless summer rains, it became a magic, mysterious scent, nearly overwhelming in its muskiness. It was the smell of youth and life and maybe the rutting of man.

Whatever it was, it held something special for those who had lived with it. Even when dry and powdery, as on that early spring morning, its scent was a comfort.

"It's good, isn't it, pard," Smokey said.

"Yes. Damn good."

It really was. My thoughts in the quiet times had been of Jan, and with those children I left back in the city. The early mornings now, the times when I got up and stumbled from Ross's bunkhouse into the house for coffee, these times were now haunted by the look of a sleepy smile and the feel of a warm arm across my chest. I remembered reading to the children while they'd fidget. I could too clearly remember the exciting smoothness of Jan's skin, those flanks of hers as trim as an antelope's.

There was a haunting there, and there would always be a haunting there, I knew, until I got back and put this trip behind me. But this morning, this first morning, this morning headed toward the mysterious black Cosos, this was the first morning that made any sense. And it hurt me that it made sense. It shouldn't make sense. I was a deserter. I tried telling myself this was simply a well-earned vacation coupled with a favor I owed my buddy during whatever time he had left. To be honest, I even considered the nobility this horseback jaunt would confer upon me. The headline in Heaven would read "Selfless Overpaid Editor Turns Back on Success to Comfort Friend."

But the headline had no zip, no real stuff. It didn't sing. I wouldn't grab it off the rack no matter what.

This morning we had been gone a week. Yes, a whole week. Well, there were things that needed doing around the ranch, of course, and hell, we hadn't seen those town people in a long time, either. We had to get used to those horses a little bit, naturally, and then there was some fence down out in the Eight Mile pasture. Can't expect Old Grant to be hauling rocks and setting dead men and brace posts. These things take time.

And there were the phone calls, too. I didn't want to get off into the Cosos until I'd made a few phone calls. I called every evening until, I think, Wednesday, and then Jan said she needed time to think about things and wished I wouldn't call for a while. She said I could write her and say what I had to say in a letter.

But I called last night again, anyway. I knew we'd be leaving before daylight. She'd gotten one of those answering machines. You know, "This is Jan. I'm not here right now..."

And then it beeped and I stayed there on the pay phone listening to the silence and thinking that she didn't say Buck and Jan aren't here. And I thought about that and tried to think of what to say, but it started to become anger instead of just hurt, and I wanted to kick something or break an answering machine or hug the kids or cry or something, so I just stood there in a phone booth on a sweet and hot evening in a little ranching town. I stood there holding this phone and looking stupid and not saying anything and then I hung up. She'd probably know who it was, too.

So this morning, when all the familiar sounds of the hooves stomping up into the stock truck came to me, and when the smells of the desert came to me and the grin of my old pard came to me, I damned myself to hell forever because I enjoyed it.

To hell with the noble stuff. To hell with the well-earned vacation stuff. To hell with Ross-needs-us-for-a-while stuff.

You're a phony, Buck. A damned-to-hell phony who maybe... no not maybe... should have gotten old Smoke a hotel room that morning. But wouldn't that just be postponing the inevitable? Would, sooner or later, that one something emerge between you that neither of you could live with?

With some people, it's money. With others, it's cooking. With a few, it's a little irritating habit the other has. In some cases, it's a deep-seated case of missing terribly something your partner just doesn't have. But now, when people don't seem to stay married for fifty years anymore, it's as though there's this hopeful waiting.

Look, I think you're wonderful and you like me, and hey, those kids are the greatest. And they like me, too, right? And you get lonely, right? Well, I get lonely, too. We've done the bed thing and we seem to get along great that way, and I have a job and you have a job, and so should we get married and try? Hey, this one thing may eventually come up . . . you know . . . the thing we can't tolerate. But maybe it won't, Honey. Maybe this time it's going to be all right. Maybe this time we'll gradually learn about each other until we really know each other and that thing won't be there. And we'll laugh inside when we remember how scared we were to get married. And we'll still be together, watching the six o'clock news when we're seventy years old and your grandkids call me Grandpa and I'll love that so much.

So let's try it, huh? Hell, I'm scared, too. I've been through the wars and lost all of them. But I'll be brave one more time because I think you're a wonderful woman, and once you get to know me, you'll see I'm really a nice guy and you didn't have to be afraid. And when two really nice people get married and they want to make things work hard enough, won't they work? Don't they have to work?"

No. Maybe the long scales of life don't always balance that way. If we'd been married a year . . . two years. Maybe then. Maybe then she'd know. Maybe then there wouldn't be an answering machine on that phone.

But there is.

Oh damn. I'm a phony. Maybe I don't mind trading that warmth, that soft arm across my chest, for the smell of salt grass in the mornings. I do, but maybe I don't mind trading it for a while. For a little. For a few weeks to make up for twenty years without it. Because this morning the smile and the arm and the children aren't haunting me the way they should, dammit!

I'm making this trip for Buck, pure and simple. Call it irresponsible. Hell, call it anything you like. It's all true, your honor. I plead guilty to being a cowboy in the first degree and throw myself on the mercies of civilization.

Fact is, I'm glad I came. Fact is, I'm really going to enjoy the hell out of this trip. Fact is, Smokey may have simply been the catalyst in a very personal chemical brew I'd been working on for a long while. The truth is, I didn't want to die before seeing those horses again, either.

Give me what's coming to me, but let it wait for just a couple of weeks. Maybe I won't be worth anything to Jan in another couple of weeks, but I wouldn't be worth anything to anybody without having those weeks first.

I shook my head, glanced over at Smokey, and watched him juggle the thermos jug and cup on his knees as he poured me some coffee.

"Hands of a surgeon," he said, handing it to me.

"All you need now are the brains to go with it, amigo."

I let the burning liquid put the pleasant capper on a morning full of overwhelmed senses. Coffee: the overture and dessert to a perfect morning.

That yellow desert dawn light was creeping up on us from the direction of Death Valley a few minutes later. Like everything else in this dry land, dawn and dark didn't mess around with foreplay. This was God's original home for simplicity and directness. You were either alive or dead, you were rich or poor. In the desert it was either brassy hot or bone-drubbing cold, parched or flooded. So okay, it was dark for the night, now it was time for daylight. Just get back out of the way and let's do it. Out here there was no poetic pretense about dawn sidling up to the darkness, holding celestial hands with it, and then gently nudging it out of the way. That was for sissy country. When dawn came here, it just flat *arrived* and then it was daytime, thank you very much.

But for those few minutes ... those very few minutes of transition, the desert became almost sacred.

"Stop the truck!" Smokey yelled.

I slammed on the brakes and damn near put Chuckles and Duster in the cab with us.

Smokey stepped slowly from the truck, spread his arms to the morning sun, and threw back his head.

"Eeeeeeee-Haaaaaaa!" he yelled, then grinned at me.

"Get your butt out here and try it, sobersides. It's good for you."

So I did, and it was. And I grinned all the way through the sleepy remains of Darwin and up the canyon into the crisp spring morning of the Coso Mountains.

Chapter Ten

GOD, BUT IT WAS FINE to see my saddle on that good bay horse. His massive neck swelled proudly up from the flat-topped horn of it. Chuckles danced around some while I tied on the saddlebags and fitted the bedroll and duffel bag on. Smokey was doing the same thing to Duster and added the gunnysack of utensils to what he had already hung on the horn.

Duster sniffed the rattling mess, got a mess of rollers going in his nose, and spooked.

"You'd better let me take those pans, pard," I said. "That pony'll drive your ugly head in the dirt."

"Look to your ownself, city boy," he yelled and stepped on. Duster made three nervous trotting steps, with that silverware sounding like a Salvation Army tambourine ensemble backed up by Satan's spurs, then he could stand it no longer. He made the mountains roar with his beller as he bogged his head and blew.

"Yee! Git 'em!" Smokey yelled.

"Ride a horse!" I shouted.

Chuckles and I loped along behind this portable rodeo for the entire three jumps it lasted, looking to pick up any survivors, but we weren't needed. That sabino stopped and looked back at the sack once, blew contemptuous snot all over it, then put his ears up and walked on up the slope away from the stock truck.

"I didn't know you could still ride bucking horses, Smoke, old as you are."

"All in a day's work for a *real* cowboy, city boy," he said, grinning. "You want I should kinda let my boot slide over and sorta goose old Chuckles there and see how you do?"

"Hell no. I've never met a horse that couldn't buck me off if he set his mind on it."

"I have," Smokey said. "Seen a few pretty good ones try, too."

I let that compliment ride along in my shirt pocket for a while, and it felt pretty good, like sunshine.

I sat there enjoying the feel of a powerful horse moving smoothly up a mountain once more. I really couldn't help making that indecent gesture to the sign warning us not to trespass. I grinned as I rode on by. By God we were going on. To what, who knew? But we were going.

It was nearing noon when we reached the little lip above the falls. Smokey held the horses while I walked down and scouted the pool of water for tracks. Horses had been here. They had either been here plenty of times, or there had been plenty of horses. I'm a fair country tracker, but I'm not good enough to tell that kind of difference in soft sand. Nothing in the sign looked fresher than several days, though. The little pool of water was clear, having had ample time to refresh itself after the horses moved on.

"They're using it all right," I said, taking Chuckles's reins and leading him down to drink, "but they're working some other water even more right now."

"Knowed 'em to do that a lot," Smokey said as we unsaddled and stashed our grub high on a rock above the pool. "They probably grazed it off here, but maybe not. Those wild horses can be just like people, I think. You know how you'll have a favorite bar and you go in and you know everybody and all them people always say the same things to each other and it feels comfortable. But then sometimes you go to another one. Hell, beer tastes the same everywhere you go, but maybe you just want to look at somebody new or maybe get in a fight with somebody you don't know, so you go to this new place for a change. I think horses just do the same thing."

"Why Smokey old man, you're a philosopher."

"You go to hell, too."

After a cold lunch, we lay back on our bedrolls and smoked and just watched the clouds hum around up there doing their cloud-type things for a while. Our horses quietly cropped the short grass that was starting to ring the pool and we just kind of let that sound sink in good. It was darned peaceful.

"Well, pard," I finally said, "how do you want to do this?"

"Do what?"

"Catch wild horses. Find Nature's snot blowers and render them gently into polite society . . . locate wolfy knotheads and turn them into gentle American citizens. Don't you think we need some kind of a plan?"

Smokey thought that over for a while.

"Buck, when you're right, you're right. We need a plan. What's your ideas on this?"

"Me? The city boy? Hell, I thought you were the wild horse catcher from who-flung-the-chunk."

"Oh, I am, I am. It's just that I like to consider all proposals before deciding . . . you know, like a chairman of the board."

I looked at him kind of funny, I guess.

"Hell," I said, "it's been so long since I've been up here. I was just a kid then, really, with Hap and old Slim."

"Aw hell, we're still just kids, Buck. Am I right? Don't you feel it? Aren't we still kids?"

I stared at the gray streaks in his hair and just laughed.

"When you're right, you're right," I said.

"Well," Smokey said, "it's like this old gold miner once told this here kid when the kid asked him how to be a gold miner, and this old guy, he just looks at this dumb kid and says, 'Hell, it's the easiest thing in the world to be a gold miner, kid. All you have to do is go to where there's gold, then bring it back and sell it.'"

I laughed. "So we just ride out to where the horses are, ask them nicely to follow us back to Ross's truck, then take them to town and sell them?"

"Amen, brother. Say, I tell you what let's do, Buck. We need to scout these mountains pretty good for these ponies first, so why don't we split up and meet back here before dark? You remember how to get to Cow Springs, right? So you ride over there and see what's going on, and I'll go down along the west ridge to that round spring."

"Sounds good to me."

It took the best part of a three-hour ride to get to the springs, and I admit to enjoying every minute of it. Chuckles stepped right out now that he didn't have to pack our camp gear, and that horse could move nice and smooth. Just for something to do, I shook out a loop and took a few little practice swings, and that bay horse came alive. His legs became springs, his ears worked back and forth and he breathed loudly. His radar was up and running, searching for anything resembling a cow to catch. I grinned and talked him down. This was definitely a roping horse.

Time plays tricks on a man. It can make a huge mountain range seem rather compact, with the valleys and canyons like rooms in a house, its passes like doors, its trails as small and personal as hallways in his mind. That's why I started thinking we'd come across Cow Springs about a good hour before we actually did. Then, when we finally got there, it took me by surprise. We were just about to top another of those interminable lava humps when Chuckles suddenly stopped, snorted slowly, and threw both ears forward. I whispered to him as I slipped the strap hobbles on him and tied him to a frail sage stem. Then I found the binoculars in the saddlebags and crawled on up to the rise.

Six horses stood there by the pool, all of them stiff like brass, all staring straight at me. There were two young mares with babies along with two older mares. The babies were pretty young, and I could guess what had happened.

When a mare is about to foal, she leaves the herd and goes off with just a nurse mare along to protect her. Stallions and some mares have been known to attack newborn foals out of jealousy, and the mares take this precaution for several days until the baby can run with its mother. These two young mothers and their nannies had decided to team up for another day or so before rejoining the herd.

These were good horses, too. They wore good flesh despite the newness of the grass.

For a few seconds we all just froze there in one of those encounters that big-game hunters come to know and cherish. The predator and the prey, face-to-face, eye-to-eye.

We are predators. Like the lion's and the wolf's, our eyes face forward so we may hunt. The horses are born prey. Like the rabbit's and the deer's, their eyes are on the sides of their heads for better peripheral vision. When the two meet in an unbounded mountain range, it is a solemn and frantic moment, and it is over too soon.

These six horses had nothing to fear from us. The nurse mares were too old, the babies too young, and the young mares would be left alone so they could care for their foals. If it came down to a choice, the foals were always roped first, anyway, as they can't live in the wild without their mothers. But we wanted young adult horses to sell, not some babies who would have to be bottle fed and pampered for six months.

The crisp desert breeze that had been brushing my face now swung around until I could feel it sweep the back of my neck under the hat brim. That was enough. The horses caught my scent and vanished.

I rode Chuckles down to the spring, loosened his cinch, and let him drink. His ears still worked hard and his eyes kept watching. He knew what had been here just ahead of him.

There was one dead snake, two dead rats of some kind, and some brush cluttering the pool. The bottom held a good collection of empty beer cans, despite its being nearly in the center of the bombing range. It took most of half an hour to clean out the shallow spring.

I cinched up and turned Chuckles toward camp, and he backtracked himself unerringly. The sun had ducked behind the Sierra massif by this time, starting that cool night breeze when we reached the falls. I had a good fire going and dinner started before I heard Smokey singing his way back down the west ridge.

Chapter Eleven

"I COME A-RINKUM DINKUM DUNKEM, I come a-rinkum dinkum doo . . . I come a rinkum dinkum dunkem . . . BUCKSTER! I've seen em, Buck! Large swatches of 'em. Entire portfolios of 'em. Gallons and gallons of wild horses. Whooooeeee!" Smokey stepped down from Duster and pulled the saddle as he talked, then grained the horse and rubbed him down.

"Must've been two hundred head, Buck, I swear. You see any?"

I told him of my afternoon's ride and my encounter with the mustang nursery.

"Well, I think I found the main constabulary of 'em over by the round spring on the west side. Lots of babies. Everybody fat as hell. There's some good-looking stuff out there."

We ate and talked and I noticed that Smokey moved slowly when he walked anywhere, as did I.

"How long you been off a horse now, Smoke?"

"Couple of months. Why?"

I chuckled. "You look as sore as I do."

"Sore, hell," he said. "You ain't sore. Once a cowboy gets broke in, 'long about when he's hip-high to a pencil stub, why he just never gets sore again. I never get sore."

"Why do I hurt so badly, then?"

"You ain't sore," he grinned. "You're just old."

That little sage cooking fire was just what we needed. In its coals we looked for something we needed and found it. A family of coyotes began yapping somewhere off to the west along a ridge. When the puppies tried their voices, we just had to laugh at their efforts. The embers of the sage roots and the baby coyotes reminded me of the ironic tenderness men in the roughest professions feel toward babies. Any babies. Perhaps this caring comes from seeing something that isn't yet covered with scars and wisdom and is still trusting.

It was that way when Smokey met Kitten.

That first time, let's see, I guess it was about in the middle of August that year. There was one night when we learned that neither of us had to go in the mountains the next morning. This happened maybe twice in a summer season, so a man learned to take advantage of it.

We had gotten to Bishop just after dark and asked around. Some kid at the gas station said the high school was having a dance, so we drove over to the high school parking lot and listened to the music from the truck.

"Wanna go in?" Smokey asked.

"No," I said, "I'll just wait here."

Through the open doors, drifting out under the cottonwoods and locusts, came the music of Chuck Berry, butchered by four local kids with electronic instruments.

"You just going to sit here?"

"Might as well," I said. The final days of high school were two years behind me then, and I knew the kind of reputation packers have with town folks. Especially in summer. "Smokey, I'm not sure this was a good idea. I don't think we'd be too welcome in there."

"Well, hell, it has to be a public dance. It's summer vacation. I'm going in. You wait here if you want to."

To my surprise, he was gone more than an hour. I walked around out in the moonlight under the trees and sat near a friendly irrigation ditch and just smelled the alfalfa coming up for its third cutting.

When Smokey came out, he had a girl hanging on him and giggling.

"Buck, this here's . . . what's your name again, Honey?"

"Kitten."

"Kitten? Your name is Kitten?"

She nodded and giggled a little more.

"Well then, Kitten, meet my pard, Buck. Ol' Buck here is the best packer and mule shoer in the entire High Sierra country because it's the grandest thing a man can do, and someday old folks and babies will whisper his name as they pass by his statue. Now Buck, I was just telling Kitty here . . ."

"Kitten," she corrected.

"I was just telling Kitten here that you have to go downtown and sit with a sick friend tonight at the Rainbow Club, ain't that right, Buck?"

"Uh, yeah. Sure do."

"Hell, that's a shame, too, pard. We was hopin' you could go for a little drive with us, but we understand, don't we, Kitten?"

She nodded and giggled.

We packed into the pickup and Smokey popped beers for the two of them. Kitten was between us and she smelled of Rexall Drug Store perfume and warm girl.

Smokey picked me up in front of the Rainbow about a half hour after closing time and we drove back to the pack station.

"She's kinda cute, Smoke."

"Huh?"

"Cute. What's-her-name, you know."

"Oh," he said. "You mean Kitten."

"Yeah, Kitten."

"Funny thing," he said. "Kitten's just a nickname, you know? Her real name is Claudia Jean Semple. She's a senior this year. She lives over on Inyo Drive. Nice two-story house. Her daddy runs the hardware store."

"What kind of grades did she get last spring?" I asked.

"Mostly Cs," he said, "but she got an A in home economics. She likes to cook and makes all her own clothes."

"Good grief, Smoke! When's the wedding?"

"Uh, what?"

"The wedding. Hell, I never knew you to learn that much about a girl on a date before. When you getting married?"

"Hey," he said, grinning, "don't be stupid. It's nothing like that."

"So you just went down to the river and had a good time, right?"

"Well . . . it wasn't just like that. Not exactly."

"Sounds like the two of you've been talking for the last five hours."

"So what's wrong with talkin'?"

"Nothing, Smoke. Not one single damn thing." I couldn't help chuckling. "Hell, there's a moon tonight, and you had some beer and that quiet stretch along the river, and a blanket over in the pickup bed and a pretty girl who giggles a lot. Sounds to me like a perfect time for conversation. You know, sort out all the world's problems, that kinda stuff."

"Well, hell, what would you have done?"

"I'm such a sorry mess with girls, I probably would've talked for five hours, pard. But I ain't you, am I?"

"Sometimes it's good just to talk, you know?"

"Is your silver pattern registered down at the saddle shop yet?"

"What does that mean?"

I laughed. "Oh nothing, just kidding. So when are you going to see her again?"

"At the reservation dance, Labor Day."

"Hoo boy! Big date. Sounds serious."

"Aw shut up," Smokey said, grinning and punching me in the shoulder. "It's just that she's a nice girl, you know?"

"Well, pard, I guess maybe she must be pretty nice. Must be real nice."

"She is," he said, and we drove the rest of the way up the mountain in silence.

Despite the joking, when a packer took a girl to the Labor Day dance on the Paiute reservation out under the locust trees west of Bishop, it *was* a big date. There were only two big occasions in the Owens Valley in summer: the Fourth of July celebration in Independence and Labor Day in Bishop. When that was coupled with a whole summer with virtually no days off, the dance became an exceedingly big deal.

Smokey left earlier than the rest of us that year. I borrowed the pack station pickup and took two other guys up about dark. We had to park two blocks from the reservation hall, finding a place behind other pickups to park. Even that far away from the brown stucco hall, the music was clear. I thought I recognized the brutal touch of the same group that had butchered Chuck Berry's best the last time I was in Bishop, but this time they sought the total destruction of Don and Phil Everly. For the minor chord changes, they each had their own ideas and each time it came around, they tried something different. Despite this racket, the dance was in full swing, with cowboys in from the mountains and up from the desert ranches to the east dancing with the town girls and some of the reservation girls. The older Paiute women stood unmoving against the walls there, watching and tapping their feet just a little.

The older Paiute men, I knew, were out under the trees playing the stick game.

The beer flowed freely, and even the occasional deputies smiled and looked the other way when a high school kid staggered . . . as long as he was grinning. The next day, we knew, the fishermen would be gone from the high country. They would go back to the city and the office, or if they were older and we'd seen them all summer, they would be hooking up the trailer and going to the Salton Sea or Yuma soon.

The cattle would soon come down the canyons, driven lazily like a bawling snake toward the winter pastures below. Some of the sporting goods stores would close, and others would go to regular hours and begin closing at night. The packers would go back to high school or college. The older ones would be moving soon to Death Valley or Wickenburg to wrangle dudes for a long balmy winter season. In a week, the mules and horses would have their shoes pulled and be turned out into valley pastures for nine months.

Labor Day was the end of the high country's mini-year. If the people in the towns and in the tiny pack stations tucked deep behind the massive canyon walls hadn't made enough money to winter on, maybe someone else would be living there when the snow went away next spring.

For three days and nights, behavior that was not normally acceptable in Bishop was expected and tolerated as long as no one got hurt too badly while doing it.

Smokey and Kitten came into the hall, danced—two slow ones—then went outside and sat on the concrete ramparts that used to be the porch in the days when the reservation hall was the separate school for Indian kids. They didn't seem to be able to see or hear anyone else, so I didn't bother them. And there was something about them that made me lonely, so I walked out and strolled along under the stars and felt the delicious warmth of a high desert night in summer.

Summer days in the desert are hard on people and animals, but the evenings atone for it. They are the kind of nights that print a memory on you forever and let you dredge it back when you need it, like the sweet smell of the warm alfalfa fields or the tart taste of the salt grass on the breeze. And each time you sit there on a desert summer night, it brings back all the other desert summer nights to you, and it accumulates with each one until after several summers in the desert at night, you want nothing to disturb the soft summer song of the night, and after ten years of desert summer nights, you sometimes find yourself crying softly and you won't know why, and after a lifetime of summer nights in the desert, you know things no man has ever been smart enough to put in books.

There was something about the stick game that seemed to fit with the night. You could hear the whack of the beater sticks and the chanting of the old men down the lane and across the parking lot to where the electric lights hung on strings between the trees and the ladies sold tamales and soda pop at card tables. A campfire burned on the other side of the stick game, and some of the single young men tended it, even though no one needed its warmth.

And up from the sitting figures came the old Paiute symphony, rising like a comforting crescendo through the syncopation of the beater sticks.

"Ah—ya- ya- WAY—y—y—ah—HAY—a—a—yah—yah—WAY..."

Old Green Hat had the sticks, and it made me smile to see him. In all the years, I never learned his name, but somehow it was more fun to think of him as Old Green Hat. Where Indians found Stetsons that color, only God can say. They weren't sold in stores. And Old Greet Hat was in fine form.

As his team of four faced the others across the blanket on the ground, he rolled his hands open slowly, tauntingly, showing one short wooden dowel to be plain, the other having the piece of black tape around its middle. Then he stuck both hands beneath the blanket and chanted loudly while his team members slapped the sticks on the long branch in front of them. Two of the other team borrowed more money from relatives and threw it into the center of the blanket, where it was quickly covered by Green Hat's bunch.

Captain Green Hat stuck both his hands beneath the blanket out of sight and moved those hands tantalizingly as he switched the dowels back and forth between his hands as the chant grew in intensity. Then Green Hat folded his arms with the dowels hidden in each fist, and he took great breaths in time to the music—ah- HUH . . . ah—HUH . . . ah—HUH—as he rocked back and forth and grinned at the other team.

This was an outright dare to the other side, and finally the oldest man sitting across the blanket picked up a beater stick and waved toward Green Hat's right hand. Green Hat kept huffing and grinning and the old man waved again toward the right hand of his cocky opponent.

"Let's see it," he said.

Green Hat grinned more, and now the whole team was swaying with him. "Ah—ya—ya—WAY. . . . Ah—ya—ya—no—way—nee—HAY . . ."

And the song and the beating of the sticks made people there think of very old things they couldn't remember.

"Let's see it, dammit!"

Then, with great ceremony, Old Green Hat unfolded his arms until both fists were just above the pile of money in the center of the blanket, and kept swaying.

The three beaters on his team went into a higher register then, and the beater sticks increased the tempo and then there was a sudden silence.

Green Hat slowly opened his right hand, and the dowel in it was the one without tape. He showed the taped dowel in the left hand. There were yips of delight from family members standing behind Green Hat's team.

"I'm a sneaky old sonofabitch, ain't I?" he said, and scooped up the money from the blanket.

There was a break then while family members passed the men beer, and Green Hat handed the dowels to the other side for their turn. One team member across the blanket quietly passed out, and his place was taken by his grown daughter. In a few seconds, the chanting began again, a haunting song of the locust grove, and this time with a woman's voice in it, too. Five-dollar bills began gathering in the center of the blanket as the players got their bets down, and the ceremonial gambling began all over again.

I bought two tamales at the card table, then walked over to the soda pop table, where I recognized Mrs. Thompson, the mother of one of the girls I had gone to school with down in Independence. They were of the Paiute band who lived at the site of old Fort Independence, two miles north of town.

"Hello, Buck," she said, smiling and handing me a pop. "Having a good time?"

"It's a great night, Mrs. Thompson. What's Marie doing these days?"

"She got married, you know."

"Hey, that's wonderful. I hadn't heard."

"Married a boy from Lone Pine . . . Tommy Pritchard . . . do you know him?"

"Well, not really, but I think I played basketball against him and got beaten pretty badly."

She laughed with that soft voice that only Indian women have and that makes a man feel just a little lonelier than he already is.

"They'll be having a baby by Christmas, Buck."

"Say, that's fine. Real fine. You give them both my best, will you, Mrs. Thompson?"

"I'd be glad to."

I walked back to the dance and just sat on the concrete steps for a while. Why is it that bands have a harder time with slow numbers than with the fast ones? Doesn't make much sense. They were dissecting some of Johnny Mathis's snuggling music this time.

After a few songs, I went in and danced with a few high school girls and one college girl home on vacation. Smokey and Kitten were nowhere around. The girls at the dance were nice, but nothing like the dark-haired girl in my daydreams, so it didn't really count.

I couldn't tell you what I expected. A girl would approach me, maybe, wearing a sign that said, "I'm Buck's future true love. Have you seen him? Are *you* Buck?" And then I'd say, "Oh, there you are. Might as well get acquainted before we get married and start planning for grandchildren." The dumb things a young guy thinks.

And you wanted to talk seriously to these girls, to sound them out, to see if they have that kind heart. To see if they could have the kindness to put up with someone like me for fifty years. But the band drowned any conversation, so about all you could tell from meeting a girl at the dance was if she was pretty, if she had a nice smile, if she'd dance with you even though she was hoping for someone else to ask her, and if she had a nice figure. It was a stupid game, but a fun game on the surface, with hopes that someday it could be the start of a serious game. And it was something you couldn't talk about with anyone, not even your pard, because you never talked about girls seriously. It was against the rules.

The morning was just starting to outline the trees when I got a full pickup truck and drove what was left of the bunkhouse crew back to the pack station. Smokey's pickup wasn't there.

About a week later we learned that Smokey and Claudia Jean Semple were getting married over the pass in Nevada about the same time the sun came over the Inyos that sleepy, magic morning.

Chapter Twelve

MY HAND REACHED OUT and touched something cold and damp and then I smiled even before my eyes opened as I recognized the rough texture of my canvas bedroll and the tiny drops of spring dew on it.

It was pink over to the east—I thought those high mountains must be the Panamints—and you could see and it was very still. Both horses were lying down now, having exhausted all the grass they could reach on the picket ropes, and there wasn't a sound from Smokey's bedroll.

Smoke still curled from the ashes of our fire, and I knew that if I rustled around with some fresh wood and fanned it a little with my hat, we'd have a breakfast fire without using a match.

But it was cold out there.

And it was warm in that bedroll. I stretched my legs out and wiggled around, and it was warm in every corner of that bedroll. And it would be warm standing by that fire, too. If Smokey would just get up and put some wood on it.

"Hey lazybones," I said.

"Not me, city man," came the muffled answer. "I can outwait anyone."

"You know you can't," I said. "Not with that terrible urgency you have."

"Terrible urgency? Never. You know you have to pee, Buck, so why don't you just get up and do it? And fix the breakfast fire while you're up."

"Hell, Smoke, I could lie here all day. But you, my friend ... ah, that's a different story. Out there just beyond that friendly bush are acres and acres of thirsty sand, parched sand, sandy sand, waiting, just waiting for that life-giving drink ..."

"Not this kid. Why, I've got a bladder that could hold back Niagara Falls, kidneys made of cast iron that can pass restrooms by through two six packs of Oly."

"The simmering sands await you," I sang in a ghostly wail. "Hear them crying, 'Smokey, here I am, sitting in a soothing setting while you seethe sorely from the direction of the setting sun.'"

"Oh cripes!" he yelled and went hopping through the brush in bare feet and long johns. "I'll get you ... ouch, damn! ... I'll get you for this ... Oh, ow, ow ..."

"And put the coffee on while you're up, Smoke," I yelled and then grinned and snuggled in until the fire got warm enough.

Those first days were sore days. Slow days. Remembering days. We'd move the pickets to put Chuckles and Duster on fat grass, and we'd water them often. But mostly we sat and talked ... of old days and good things and maybe just a touch or two of friendly slander.

But every day we rode. At first we rode only an hour or two and then spent the rest of the day stretching and moving slowly and asking ourselves questions about sanity.

Smokey recovered in about four days, but it took me more than a week. Maybe it was two weeks. We weren't counting by then. City life plays dirty tricks on a cowboy. The body that was once tuned to a horse now sat astride with a stupid expression asking, "Just what the hell is this you expect me to do?"

But Chuckles was a gentle, patient partner. As we'd lope off across the sagebrush, he forgave the floppiness and miscues as we grew to learn each other. Chuckles lost his grass belly and got back into shape before I did. He breathed more easily on our daily lopes over the hills. In a short time, he'd tuned himself into a running machine.

And as my muscles and mind gradually switched over to horseback, I really began to appreciate this bay horse. I'd never ridden a horse that was as smooth through rock piles and the sage flats. He flowed over and around obstacles. And, to my everlasting shock, about a week or so later, I began to flow with him.

What happens is inexplicable and deserves a few moments' consideration. There is a memory built into the mind and the muscles that, once learned, never disappears. There comes a moment that good horsemen learn, when you cease being man and horse and become a traveling unit. When it happens, it is a wondrous thing. You can sit back and remember the feeling again and again in later years when all you ride is a pickup truck.

You learn the way the horse thinks and how he moves, and how far each leg moves on each stride and just where he'll put his feet. And a lot of it depends on how long his legs are and how flat or steep the terrain may be. You can look down, in the early stages, and *know* just where the right hoof will go and where the left hoof will go. Just ahead of that rock with the right, and just short of that clump of grass with the left. And later in this early stage, you'll begin to know by feel where those hind legs are going to touch down. And when those massive hindquarters give a heave up over a log, you are with him and you know it. Because you *know* it.

Then, after many hours in the saddle over long days, and if you have spent years riding in your youth, you can pick up once again the rhythm of the horse. Not just any horse, but this nice bay, Chuckles. No two horses will run a dodging pattern through sagebrush the same. It may look the same to someone who is watching, but not to the rider in the saddle. Each horse's way of traveling is like a fingerprint. Blindfolded, and at any gait, you will be able to tell your horse from others.

Finally, your unstretched muscles limber up and begin to fit the saddle and the horse. As this happens, you can begin to feel the horse beneath you as an extension of yourself and not an alien being whose back you are on for transportation.

Finally, when the horse is let out into a run, your muscles flex along and you sense, rather than see, the changes in the ground beneath you. When the horse strains over an obstacle, your body strains with it, shifting to put your body where it will do the horse the most good. And these reflexes happen ten times to a second, twenty or fifty times to a second, until there is just one being with two brains moving through the brush, with one brain telegraphing movement to the other, and the other sending body signals to the first. And one says where you'll go, and the other says how you'll go, and the two just go and flow, like some primordial fugue, with the messages chasing each other and complementing each other and all of it making sense and a spooky kind of poetry at the same time.

That's what happens when it's good.

We rode that way, looking over the country for a week and more than a week. We watched the wild horses, although we knew we didn't have to. And we scouted the country and looked in old abandoned mines and killed a few snakes. And twice we ducked into deep ravines when we heard the scream of the jets, and then we came out again.

One day, while riding alone, I stopped up on a ridge where I could see the Sierra peaks, and I stepped off and sat on a rock and just watched the peaks. Sometimes it helped.

See those peaks? Nothing you will do in your lifetime will affect them. Nothing anyone has done in millions of lifetimes has affected them. Your personal problems are no more to them than the burrow of a marmot in one of their myriad rockslides. Less than that. Whether I have a happy life, or a short life, or a miserable life, or no life at all won't change this particular view. Ever.

We may be less than nothing, but we have dreams, and dreams are something rocks and peaks are denied. Mine came again, there on that rock with the magnificence of the mountain range spread before me. Jan's smile on Jan's face framed by blond hair, and she was saying she was on my side, and there was nothing we couldn't do together. But then she went into the bathroom in my daydream and started crying. I talked to her and talked to her, and finally she said she'd come out and everything would be all right, and the door opened and she came out. But she had dark hair now, and her face wasn't Jan's face. It was the same face of the dark-haired girl of my youth dreams, and she said everything would be fine and we'd be together, and I got angry because she had replaced Jan, and it wasn't fair to Jan.

Jan was still crying in the bathroom; I could just hear her in the background, and I had no right to see the dark-haired girl. Not anymore. It was just wrong.

During these days, the hardest work was fixing up the old mustanger's corral about three miles from camp. Wind and neglect had knocked most of it down, and that sometimes meant riding a great distance to find dead branches to strengthen it.

The only good thing about fixing up that old corral was feeling the difference in our muscles as the days went by, gradually getting warmer as the sun pushed along toward the inevitable blast that is summer.

There was something else happening, too. There comes a nice feeling one day when you swing up into the saddle more easily, because either you don't weigh as much as you did, or you're just stronger than you were, and it doesn't matter a damn which. Then, too, old forgotten smells and textures return. Your boots become used to the weight of the large, gentle California spurs, and your ears pick up the familiar chiming of the rowels as you walk. The chaps take on that particular hang they used to have until it feels right for you to have them on and just a little bit naked when you take them off. Your hat has always fit right.

It was good relearning the smells, too. Like the honest sweat of work in the sun. It came to have a familiar feel to it, and I discovered I wasn't running to the falls to wash twice a day. Even if I ate with dusty hands, no undue poisoning occurred. In fact, I realized I felt pretty good.

And as the days went along, I began to notice the texture of the mountains around me and thought less and less of the news that was undoubtedly taking place all over the world.

Somewhere out there, banks were being robbed and babies born and terrorists killing people and governments forming and toppling, and none of them required my immediate attention. I hadn't taken a pill in a long time, now, and began to wonder why I ever had.

I rode hard enough during the day now that I dropped to sleep almost immediately after pulling off my boots and sliding into the chilly bedroll. About the time my own body heat made the bedroll warm enough to unclench my muscles, my mind unclenched as well until morning. I didn't want time to think. Not at night. Horses owned me during the day, but Jan owned my nights and that precious time just before I got up to fix the fire. I kept telling myself there wasn't one single damn thing I could do about Jan out here in the middle of the

Coso Range and tried to concentrate on other things, but that didn't always work.

Would she still be there when this was over? And, as I had recently begun asking myself, was it even remotely possible that Jan might enjoy living in this ranch country? But I was smart enough not to tell myself the answer. Jan was now the girl in the dream. That precious one who kept a man company in his alone time. The dream girl now had blond hair and children and lived in a white house Down Below. The smile, the love, came from a face framed by blond hair. It made me feel good to know that. There was a name and address now with the dream. The dark-haired girl had no business there anymore, and I only occasionally saw the dark-haired girl.

It had to be enough, right then, to let the mountains become part of me and shape me back into a child of its wild canyons. The fine dust of the alkali flats began to coat things with its graphitic touch and make my chaps polish my saddle and my saddle polish my chaps.

Everything seemed to fit. One lazy afternoon we'd been out looking over a small valley full of horses and taking turns watching the flying-saucer-shaped Sierra wave clouds twist themselves into stratospheric ghosts. When the coolness of the late afternoon came, we silently got on our horses and rode back toward camp. It had to be a good three miles back, and suddenly Smokey put the spurs to Duster and the sabino flew like a bat through the sagebrush. Chuckles wanted to run, so I let him, and we were sailing along through occasional war whoops down the long, gentle ridge swells toward camp.

Duster went wide around a rock pile and Chuckles flew over it and made up the difference, and then we were side by side racing along, the horses breathing easily and straining good-naturedly in the race.

I looked across at Smokey and we grinned at each other and yelled a few more times, and then we were quiet, just flowing with the pounding run of our horses and watching the sage get sucked up beneath those churning pistons.

It seemed, too, with the frantic pounding of the hooves, that the mountain picked up the counterpoint and gave us some music to listen to with a silent inner ear. It wasn't the flash and fire of Rossini, but the soft morning music of the Impressionists. Debussy in the desert, Ravel through the ravines. It was a haunting song born of the earth and the mountain and wild things and it swelled up slowly to that hidden ear and soothed in contrast to the heavy pace of the running horses. It was the kind of song that makes a man think perhaps he's losing his mind just a little, but it's so pretty he doesn't care. I had heard it before, but not for a long time.

It ended when I pulled Chuckles up just short of camp, and we watched as Smokey and Duster went skittering through the camp, jumping the fire pit and then sliding to a stop beyond.

We walked the horses together down an arroyo to let them blow; then I took Duster's reins so Smokey could rustle us up a dinner fire.

"Pard?" I said.

"Yeah?"

"I've got my seat back."

"Aw hell, Buck." He grinned. "Never thought you'd lost it."

Chapter Thirteen

WORKING WITH WIRE GRIPES THE SOUL and chokes off creativity. It also hurts your hands.

We had pulled and straightened and redriven all the nails we could find down at the old horse pens, and that left a lot of corral still to be built and nothing but wire to build it with. I managed to mention several times that wire wasn't my favorite artistic medium as I twisted my thumb in another loop of it again. Smokey just grinned.

"Nothing like this Mormon silk for fixin' fence, is there?" he said. "I'd like to use haywire on the guy who thought this up. And then I'd like to use barbed wire on the guy what invented that stuff. And then I'd like to run flat over the idiot who invented the tractor and the baler and the hay wagon. Then, you see, I'd like to take that damned chicken wire and wrap it around the neck of the chicken farmer sumbitch who came up with that horse-cripplin' crap."

He grinned in a philosophical kind of way.

"It's all a plot, Buck. It's a plot to get a guy off a horse and turn him into a farmer. Now bein' a farmer's okay, if you don't know no better, or if you're one of those guys who likes to walk around and feed pigs and gather eggs. Nothing against them. But a man needs to ride a horse and chase cows and throw a rope or he just kinda goozles down into a pillow-shaped thing that don't know from squat. When they make the job more complicated with feeding chickens and milking cows and fixing fence and swamping out water troughs, well . . . it may be work, but it sure as hell ain't cowboyin."

The juniper branches were rough, and it was tougher wrapping them with wire and cinching them tight with a twisting stick than either of us had expected. The work had been going on for better than a week, but we could only bring ourselves to do this kind of work for maybe an hour a day. Add it all up; it was maybe two full days and another half or so. But at last we had a handle on it and it looked to be pretty tight.

Smokey backed off about four steps and looked at it. It was the typical round corral of the mustanger, with sides six feet high and with branches laced through it tight enough to hold a chicken. Well, maybe a turkey.

"Is she horse-high, hog-tight, and bull-strong?" I asked.

"Only one way I know of to find out," said Smokey. And he gave a yell and ran at the back end of that corral as hard as he could.

There was a crash and the creaking and groaning of wire and wood and a great cloud of white dust puffed up from the sagebrush he smacked into. The fence gave just a little with his weight, like an antique system of springs, then it remembered where it was supposed to be and returned to that position with a violence that flopped Smokey back almost to the snubbin' post in the middle of the corral. I thought he was dead.

"Are you all right?"

"Aaaaaaargh . . ." he moaned, clutching his throat and thrashing around on the ground. "Oooooooooaaaaach. Aaaach-aaaaach."

I ran up to him and looked down at his face. Through the dust coating he had picked up from all the brush in the fence, I could just see wild eyes, his gasping mouth, and his hands clutching his throat.

"Smoke! Are you all right? What's wrong? Where are you hurt?"

He feebly motioned me closer with one hand while trying to whisper. I knelt beside him, thinking please no, not here, not now. This isn't right. I don't know what to do.

"Buck?" he whispered.

"Right here, pard."

He motioned me closer. My ear was inches from his mouth.

"Beer," he whispered.

"What's that, Smoke? I thought you said beer."

"Beer," he said, a little louder. Then he grinned up at me. "Beer! I must have beer! I'm drier'n a popcorn fart and I'll flat die if I don't have beer soon."

"You old sonofabitch!"

He just grinned and stood up. "Tell you what let's do, Buck. Let's go soak off some dirt at the hot springs, then head in to Trona for a cold one. What do you say?"

"Beats punching a time clock."

"About the grandest thing a man can do," he said, grinning.

"Better'n a redheaded woman," Smokey said, echoing my own thoughts. There might be something better than lying full length in a hot springs pool in the center of a big sagebrush flat, looking off across hellacious rocky ridges toward who-knows-what while a thunderstorm crashes around you and makes steam rise high off your pool. Maybe.

We had been immersed and soaking out a lot of soreness for about fifteen minutes when the storm came piling up from the west over the crest of the Sierra. The clouds did their slow boil as we lay in the hot water, dredging alkali dust from our bodies. Then there came the smell of a rain that made Duster and Chuckles look up from their grazing nearby on the picket ropes and flare their nostrils.

There was a cold breeze, all of a sudden, as if someone opened the door of the bathroom while we were taking baths. We slid farther into the water and savored the warmth and let the cold breeze enjoy its moment, too.

"We ought to be getting out if we're going to Trona," I said. "It's a long ride to the truck."

Smokey surfaced slowly like an old walrus with a secret clam bed. "Man ride along this ridge today, he'd get struck dead by lightning, sure as hell," he said, and started sinking again. Before the water closed over his mouth he said, "You in any big hurry?"

"No," I said, thinking about that lightning. "Now that you mention it, I didn't lose nothing in Trona."

Smokey spurted a little warm water spurt in the air and just smiled like a dog who got into the butter. "I don't care if we get there after dark. Road still runs down that way, even when you use headlights, Buck."

And I knew what he meant. I had felt a subtle shifting of gears in the past few days, a lessening of tension. We had worked and ridden and camped and built things, and the only thing that mattered to us was the weather.

Smokey looked over and grinned with that two-toned face that came from wearing a hat in the desert sun. I grinned, too, thinking that I had a two-toned face again. I hadn't seen a mirror in several weeks, but all I had to do was look at my nut-brown hands against my white arms to know what the face would surely show.

"Last time I saw Trona," Smokey said, "it occurred to me that it would look better after dark anyway. Why, the last time I was in Trona

. . . let's see . . . that was right after we went jackassin' over to Death Valley, I believe. Well anyway we went into town there and . . ."

"Shut up, Smokey! For crying out loud."

"Shut up? The man says shut up. Why?"

I grinned. "Don't you know talkin' draws lightning?"

So we just lay there in the hot pool and laughed, and when the rain came we ouched our way barefooted to the nearest brush and hung our clothes out for a good wash and stuffed our boots and valuables beneath the saddles. Then we hopped back into the pool, letting that first rush of warmth from the water sink into our muscles and bones again. And we heard the bellow of the thunder around us, watched the clouds, black as death, frame the desert ridges. We flinched with each bolt of lightning. Then we just lay there without talking as we became a very insignificant part of one of nature's greatest exhibitions. There was a feeling of being sunk in the pool and in the earth itself and watching through eyes filled with rain as somehow we became like rocks or old tough sticks, deeply rooted and bare-breasted to the lightning and the elements. It felt right.

I wondered if it would feel right to Jan, too. I wondered if she would think this was fun. I wanted desperately for this to be fun for Jan. Maybe I could take her to some legal hot springs like Dirty Sock or Big Hot, and we could time it right for a thunderstorm, and we could soak in the waters and feel close to each other. But somehow that picture didn't last, and it may have been just that it was so . . . planned. When you get caught in an adventure like this, not only does it mean more to you, but you come to treasure it because it gets stamped "memorable" and put in the memory drawer to be brought out and dusted off whenever one needs a soak in a hot springs pool during a thunderstorm.

Then, as I lay there thinking these things, I thought that maybe I thought too much, anyway. Maybe I'm the only one who mentally puts people in these situations and then guesses what would happen. You'd never know the outcome unless it just happened, anyway, and maybe I should just concentrate more on what's going on here and now.

Here and now the cool breeze took the storm east to hurl itself to lonely rags over Death Valley. Then we lay there some more until the new sun dried out our clothes on the sage.

When we were finally dressed, saddled, and riding for the truck, it was coming on dark, with the big stringers of light pouring through the mountain passes to the west like searchlights looking for freedom.

It beat taking a shower back at the ranch.

Chapter Fourteen

I HAD TO GET UP FROM THE STOOL and walk out into the night air, even the rotten-eggs night air of Trona. It had been so quiet in the mountains for so long the noises of the bar were ripping me open.

Chuckles and Duster were in the truck, and I scrambled up and talked to them for a few minutes, then got down and walked down the little road between the railroad tracks and the fringe of sand-break tamarisk and listened to the jukebox music coming from the bar.

There is a feel to Trona, a weight, a silence of heaviness and sluggishness and work. Few places make a man feel he is in the presence of work as much as Trona, California. It is one of the world's necessary places, like Suez and San Quentin and Bakersfield. It exists because men must work here. They go other places to have fun. Here they work and here they drink beer.

Trona sifts through the nostrils of the night like a sweaty whore. Out on its dry lake, the big machines scrape up the wet alkali muck and let the wind carry the smell around as a reminder of work. All for borax. All this stink and work in this hellish hot little town for borax so people can make beautiful glazes on pottery, make metal purer, and make clothes cleaner.

Bringing a brand-new baby into the world is worth the months of pregnancy and the hours of labor, but Trona is constantly in labor. Its thick, stinking soup kills the sweet desert smell of the few tamarisks. Its houses with thick green shingles have huge overhanging roofs to hide them from the constant pounding of the sun. Some locals say the swamp cooler was invented here. No town ever needed it more.

But Trona also has friendly people and beer. And the friendly people and the beer were too loud in the bar. There's something about the absence of noise that makes common sounds harsh, and I wasn't ready to go back to common sounds yet. When I finally walked back in, looking for Smokey, the beer smell blended with the whiffs of stinking desert soup on Searles Dry Lake, and the crispness of the beer made it seem heavenly by comparison.

But the country music was too loud and the people talked too loud and I just wanted to drink a beer and look at the bar things on the wall and go back to the Cosos, back to camp, back to my bedroll.

"What do you think, pard?" Smokey said, grinning. "Want to see how we can do with the local women? No? Well, how about a good fight, then? No harm in that. Not even a *little* fight? Hell, you aren't any fun at all."

Smokey looked over at me and winked. "Damn, Buck, we came here to have fun, and all you want to do is have a beer. You've got to learn to relax and enjoy stuff a little. See that woman down at the end of the bar? She's been lookin' this way. I think she's in love with you."

"What?"

"Love . . . you remember. Holding hands, moonlight walks, soft music, five-dollar motels? Love. The stuff kids are made of."

"I'm married, remember?"

"For how long? Gotcha there, didn't I? For how long? You run into an old trail pard and off you go skipping around over the mountains chasing horses and you expect her to be there when you get back? Is she that dumb?"

"No. She's not that dumb. I've been thinking about it some, too, Smoke."

"You going back when this is over?"

"I've been thinking about it, that's all."

"It looks different now, don't it?"

"Some. It looks some different now. There may not be a whole lot there to go back to when this is over."

"So how about the little lady down the bar?"

"No chance, amigo."

"She's kinda cute, in a three-beer kinda way."

"I've done dumb things all my life, but I've always been true blue to the girls. Sequential monogamy, pard. One at a time. Maybe what we've got isn't the best, and maybe it won't last out the week, but by God we've got it right now and that's worth something. No woman ever had to worry about me cheating."

Smokey looked over and grinned. And there was some pain behind his grin.

"You know my reputation, right?" he said. "Well, I got to tell you something. Now this is a four-beer thing to tell someone, but I'm telling you on three beers, so you can see I'm serious. You remember when I was married to Kitten? I never cheated on her. Never came close. I never even looked at another woman the whole time we were together. Remember I told you I got a bottle and a blonde and got over her? I lied like a rug, Buck. Like a damn rug. I got a bottle and all I got was sick. No blonde. Not for months. Not until she was going out with other guys. And sometimes I think I never got over her all the way, either. Dumb, huh?"

"Not dumb. Not dumb at all. Shows you're a man of character and depth . . ."

"Now *that's* a bunch of bull . . ."

". . . and a man of character and depth can buy his partner another beer."

"Two more here, sir," Smokey said. "I was thinking maybe this could be a good night for us. Kinda cut loose and roar a little, like the old days. We ain't roarin' much, are we?"

"Well," I said, "for one thing you thought this was Saturday and turns out it's only Thursday, that's one thing. But did we ever roar that much, Smoke? I mean really, did we ever? I remember us driving up and down the main drag of Bishop with the country music up all the way in the pickup, honking the horn at the high school girls on the sidewalk. Or we flirted with the waitresses at the Pines Café, knowing damn well we wouldn't do anything about it because we liked them too much and they liked us too much and we wouldn't want to mess up each other's lives."

"Well," he said, "how about that one night in Bishop? Down at the Rainbow Club?"

"The night you sicced the Paiute mafia on me?"

"Aha! He remembers!"

"Hard to forget that, my friend. That's like asking Custer if he remembers the day he rode into the valley of the Little Bighorn River."

Ah, it *was* a night. It was a night worth remembering and worth smiling about and tucking it away and saving it for fun, and now it was even more fun taking this one out and dusting it off and having a smile again.

I had left Smokey in the Rainbow that night to have a few beers while I drove up to see an old-timer in Round Valley. A few hours later, when I'd had all the coffee I could hold, I drove back into town to find my pard.

Now when I tell this, I have to explain that Smokey had discovered this very attractive Paiute girl at the bar and had invited her over to one of those little padded Naugahyde booths. She came over, and he was sitting there with one arm around her, sipping beer with the other hand, and telling her of the glories of seeing the sun come up over the aqueduct on an old army blanket.

And she giggled some and that started the trouble.

There were three big men in there who didn't like Smokey's overtures to this lady. He says they were her boyfriends, but in the brief moment when I saw them and her together, I'd put more money on them being her brothers. At any rate, they came to stand before the table facing the Naugahyde booth and there was Smokey, gingerly taking his arm down from this girl's shoulder and grinning that grin of his that means something's going to happen at any moment, and that something would probably be hugely sudden. His right hand, the one on the bottle of beer, was quietly turning upside down and fastening slowly around the long neck while these men mumbled drunkenly what they were going to do with Smokey, or with parts of Smokey. It basically involved pruning his immediate branch of the family tree.

At that very moment, I walked in the front door of the Rainbow Club. There were the backs of the three large men, and between them was my pard with that dumb grin on his face and the girl, still giggling, at his side.

I tried to figure the situation out, but fortunately Smokey took care of that for me.

"Why, there's my pard just coming in the front door," said *mi buen amigo*, "and it's all over for you now, fellas, 'cause he's going to kick the living owl shit out of *all of you!*"

When he said that, I remembered something I'd forgotten to leave in the truck (me) and hurried along to take care of it, with three drunks stumbling along after me the best they could. They couldn't catch me on their best day, however, as I had a whole boilerful of incentive that they just didn't have.

Smokey nipped out the back door, and we met two blocks away and laughed all the way back to the pack station.

Even years later, it seemed funny.

"That was a hoot, wasn't it?" Smokey said there in the bar in Trona, sipping his beer.

"Funny *now*, I guess. Hell, I thought you'd killed me for sure that night."

"Never," he said. "*Never!* Why, I couldn't do a thing like that. That was simply a case of becoming closer pardners. See, after that night, you can always say you saved my life, right? Hell yes. So that just makes us closer pards and that's good for everybody. You even been back in the Rainbow since that night?"

"You crazy?" I said. "Never know how good their memories for faces might be."

Smokey just grinned like always. "You know, that was the last time *I* was in there, too. Thought about going in there again, but couldn't find anyone to borrow a suit and tie from."

"Chicken-hearted bastard," I said, laughing.

"Make that '*alive* chicken-hearted bastard' and I'll throw in with you."

There it was. Alive. Damn that word.

It had been great. Living beyond our capabilities. Tuning horses and bodies up and cooking over the fire and getting away from the realities they wanted us to face, and not talking about the thing that was killing him slowly. It was like it was twenty years ago. Well, a little like it, anyway. We could still ride and still rope some, and by smash, we were sure as hell still cowboys and wild horse men and there we were forgetting about life and he said alive chicken-hearted bastard like that, and there it was, right flat in my face again.

And my beer stuck in my throat and then I looked around and wondered. This was the Oasis, in Trona. Sure. And there were the beer signs that look fascinating after you'd had a couple, and there were the old pictures on the wall, and there at the end were the snapshots of the regulars acting silly, or if they were very drunk, trying to look dignified with their eyes nearly shut. And there were always the jokes going around, but they were the same old jokes. And why was the Oasis any different from the Fairview Inn in Talkeetna or the Flame Lounge in Fairbanks or the Territorial House in Corrales or the Pines Café in Independence, or even the dumb Rainbow Club in Bishop? How was it different? It was the same stuff. People ducking in for something warm and fun, a laugh and a beer and a sip of relaxation while they were still here and to give a friend something to remember after they were dead, so that we smiled when we remembered someone and said, "Yeah, he was a good ol' boy, wasn't he? I remember the time, hell I think he sat right where you're at now..." And that was really what it was about, wasn't it?

Wild horse hunters, hell. We were just a couple of beer drinkers on a night with a moon and the sour stink of Searles Lake armpits washing through us and the breeze in the tamarisks and we wouldn't be us too much longer. We were like the sun dogs of the misty winter days, hanging out at the ends of our luminous arc, looking in at life burning in the center and not being able to hold it. We were both captive to the center and unable to approach it. And we wouldn't be *we* that much longer. It would be just me, and damn him anyway for saying that.

"I want to go back to camp, Smoke."

"Sure," he said, quietly. "Why not?"

And I knew when he said it like that, he knew, too. He knew and was thinking about it, too, and damn it hurt so bad when you were having fun.

Chapter Fifteen

WE CAN TELL WHEN THE TIME COMES. The feeling seeps in and sharpens some parts of us while it dulls others. It takes a long time to get the city out of us, like waiting out a bad hangover.

But then one day the muscles respond the way they should, the lungs get clearer, the eyes see more than they have before. There are things happening in the mind, too. Perhaps that is why someone from the city has a hard time understanding someone from the tall lonelies. And it is why someone from the plains and mountains can't understand why a man would want to live in a stucco cliff dwelling and spend all day being nervous.

There is a spell to the mountains and the desert that must be experienced alone. There is a time when the soft music starts in our minds, a soft accompaniment to life as we walk or ride around. And we find we know things we didn't know before. That part of us in a hurry to get something done is dulled, while that part of us that loves beauty and symmetry and plain old fate is heightened until we smile for no reason at all.

We become more like the animals we depend on for our lives. We feel the hills—travel over the hills lightly, like a caress—and we simply get to *know* what's ahead and what we're going to do. It's a natural feeling and it comes to those hermits and mountain men and trappers and eccentric prospectors and other coots that normal people can't understand. And it comes to wild horse hunters as well. The Indians in Alaska call it "the good feeling." Mountain men call it "walking in beauty." And with mustangers, it just means the mountains have seeped through us and the horses; the horses work as one with us; the ropes we've practiced with daily become like the "th'LIT-so-yah," the magic ropes of the Tlingit spiritual people, and work like extensions of our desires.

It means, when it comes, that we are ready. It is as simple and as complex and as mystical as that.

Perhaps because we both knew Trona was a bad idea and because we both knew it was time to put up or shut up with these wild horses, and perhaps because we both knew when we saddled up it would be to make the final chase, maybe that's why we found a reason the next morning to stay in camp and brew one pot of coffee after another.

It would be over soon enough.

"Tomorrow morning, you think?" Smokey asked.

"Bright and early. You got a plan yet?"

"I've been thinking some on that, Buck. Been thinking more and more since I've been up here. I think we could water trap a bunch of them, probably, but hell, that doesn't seem right and I wanted to ask you about it."

I looked at him and smiled. "One on one. Horse and rider after one horse at a time. Fair chase."

Smokey brightened. "You knew? Yes. Something fair. Just build a oop and spur hell for leather, and if we catch them, it's because God wanted them caught, and if we don't..."

"If we don't," I finished, "we still get a good suntan out of all this."

"And we've had a chance to ride together like we used to. You know, it's been good. It's been good being pards again."

"It has. Hasn't been like the old times, though, Smoke. Not really."

"I know what you mean. I think it's been better. It means a little more, in a way. You know what I mean?"

"I think we're both older now, and that helps."

I did the honors on coffee, then leaned back against the horse-sweat impregnated fleece of my saddle.

"When we're young, Smoke, I guess we think we're going to live forever..." I couldn't believe I'm saying this. "... and everything is either going to work out great, or we're afraid we'll end up down on skid row with a bottle of Tokay for a friend. We're a bit older now, and we've both been up the crick and over the ridge in our own ways, and we can look back along with looking forward..."

I was not going to mention death. I was not going to accept death. Not his and sure as hell not mine. Not on a day when I could move like a cat and hear everything in the world move.

"... you know, looking forward to good things. To amassing more memories. To being partners again."

Smokey looked across the fire at me with a strange look and right there at first I was afraid I'd stepped across some forbidden line. Then he grinned.

"Damn, city boy! Got to get you the hell out of these mountains before you start writing poetry. Hells bells, man, I thought we were just here to catch wild horses."

"You're right." I grinned. "It *was* getting a little heavy there for a minute."

"A little deep, you mean."

Smokey was quiet for a few minutes, then picked up a stick and started drawing brands in the sand.

"Buck, you've been around. In fact, you've been around a *lot* . . ."

"Not sure I like the sound of this," I said.

" . . . and I just wondered if you've ever really figured women out."

I laughed. "You know better than that."

"No. I'm serious. Like have you, you know, figured out what to do around them? Ah hell, you know."

"When you ask a question like that, ask it of some guy who's been married to the same woman for forty years and still likes her. Don't ask a guy like me, who's had more weddings than anniversaries."

"Well hell," he said, "they ought to give a guy a guidebook or a owner's manual or something, you know? With Kitten, I thought I had the world by the ass and was spurrin' for money, you know? At first there."

Yeah, at first it had looked pretty good. Two young people having fun with moving from one ranch to another, towing a borrowed trailer full of furniture and saddles and stuff, having fun discovering what pregnancy is all about, and this was all punctuated by the occasional rodeo to enter and a few dances in town. Laughter and love can do wonders to a beat-up mobile home at a remote cow camp.

For about two years, it had looked real good. Kitten was away from her parents and taking an interest in ranch life.

She wrote me once, even. She said she knew I was Smokey's partner and she had finally figured out what that meant, and she just wanted me to know she was making a good cowboy's wife. And she told me, with lots of ha-ha's in every paragraph, how the cows had gotten into the haystack at the barn when all the men were gone, and how she and an old heeler named Blue had put them back out in the pasture. And all this while she was seven months along. It was a good, happy letter, and it was one I needed at that time, and I knew I'd have to get up and see them before long.

During those years, I was torn between two lives. I'd go to the mountains in late spring and pack mules until all the dudes went home or back to school in the fall. By that time of year, none of us ever wanted to see another mule as long as we lived. Then, with just milking to be done, I'd get a little tired of bunkhouse talk, and I'd shave off my beard and drive around until a little weekly newspaper in a quiet town would hire me as a reporter.

All through the fall and winter I'd work in the newsroom, and I'd get to know the people in the town, and then spring would come, and the streams would be gorging fresh-blown with silt from the big canyons, and I'd know the sun was up there on Kearsarge and Sawmill and Forester and Glen and Taboose, searching through the pillowy drifts for the rocky trails it knew were down there. And I'd get to thinking about those nice mules out there in pasture, and I'd wonder if anyone was feeding Leona the hotcakes she loved so well, and I'd wonder if the quarter crack on Lady's hoof had healed up, and I'd think, too, of Coalie and Wilma. These two mules, over a winter-long courtship in winter pasture, had decided years ago to be "married" to each other. I'd wonder if they were still in love, and, if they were, what made it work for them.

And one day the sun would be shining on my neck as I walked along the little street of the little town toward the newspaper office, and all of a sudden there would come a crowding. The newspaper office, where people better than me had written and retired and died for a hundred years, seemed like a casket, and it seemed to me it was a lot of waste to work that hard just so people could see how the high school team was doing—especially since they already knew—and to learn what the theme of this year's church bazaar might be. And about that time, there would be just the hint of a message in the breeze. Just a little taste of something wild, but it was enough for two weeks' notice, or a month's notice if I really liked the boss.

Then the rented room would go back to the landlord clean, and I would use the cleaning deposit for gas and drive all night and listen to country music and sing along with it and drink coffee in good, old-fashioned coffee shops, and by the time it was morning, there would be the mountains on my left, climbing toward the sun and holding their secrets tucked away until the snow left the trails for summer. Then that breeze would whisk the sour smell of alkali dust and salt grass to me and tell me I was home.

Life being what it was, sometimes, every few years, there would be a very nice girl with me. Once it was a ranch girl I married, who left when we moved to town. Once it was a town girl I married, who left when we moved to the pack station. But both times, each of them gave the change her best shot. Bless them for that. They tried.

So when I finally got up to visit Smokey and Kitten at the old Deep Six Ranch way back over toward Nevada, I was optimistic for them. They'd been together almost four years then, and there was little Crystal, my "niece." She was a coming two-year-old by that time, and I felt good about it.

That's why it struck me so hard to learn that things might not be as smooth as I'd hoped. Like at dinner that first night. Smokey and I talked about grass and rain and colts and kids and dogs, and all the while, Kitten just sat there. I didn't want her to feel left out, so I tried to get her to talk about life on the remote ranch.

"Mary—you know Mary up at the big house," she said, "well, she's nice enough and lets me use the washing machine. With Crystal running around now, well, we need to wash clothes almost every day. If we had a washing machine, it would really help."

"You know we can't go buy you a machine," Smokey said. "Hell, we don't even have any place to put it. Mary lets you wash any time you want to."

"But it's not *our* machine," Kitten said.

"So what's the difference?"

"You wouldn't understand."

"You got *that* right," Smokey said. "You want to wash clothes, you can just go wash them and they're just as clean. Hell, let's go out for a smoke."

Smokey and I walked out by the corrals and looked around as the sage on the hillsides across the pasture turned pink with the setting sun.

"You ever heard anything like that?" Smokey said. "She can go on like that for hours now. I guess ever since Crystal was born. She wants this and wants that. What she *really* wants is to move to town so she can be with her mommy again and have her daddy find me a job and take care of us. I thought she was all grown up."

"Sorry you're having problems, pard."

"Our only problem is her. Hell, she knew what this was going to be like when we got married. She was happy as a tick until the baby was born and all of a sudden she wants to live in town and have town stuff."

"It happens that way sometimes when a woman has a baby."

"You see Chrissie? You ever see a happier kid? She loves it out here. Look at this place. Mountains and desert as far as you can see and not much barbed wire on it. Hell, she's got her own little pony to ride and she can splash in the water troughs and she just has a hell of a good time."

"She's a dandy, pard. No doubt about that."

"And I got to tell you this, Buck. Don't say nothing to anybody, but things haven't been like they were . . . well, like before . . . romantically . . . if you know what I mean."

"Yeah," I said. "I know."

Smokey rolled a smoke, taking a lot of unnecessary care to get all the tobacco strands inside before he licked it.

"It don't make any kind of damn sense at all," he said. "I mean, this is the best deal we've ever had. Kitten and her folks are always yapping about security and stuff, and Old Man Wharton's already told me I have a year-round job here for as long as I want it. We've got us a nice trailer house to live in. Two bedrooms. The saddle stock is all good. Not a jughead in the bunch. The fence almost never needs fixing. The old man doesn't care if you rope a calf now and then to keep your hand in, and we get all the beef we want. Free. You can see, can't you, Buck? She was after me to settle down, so I settled down. Okay. Here I am, settled down. Hell, I've been here almost a whole damn *year* now. I wish I knew what the hell she wanted."

"Wish I could help you," I said, and meant it.

I thought I'd leave the next day after breakfast, so I hung around for another cup of coffee after Smokey and the others had ridden off for the day.

"I'm glad you came here to see Smokey," Kitten said, refilling my cup.

I smiled. "Hey, I came here to see you and Crystal, too."

"Oh, I know, but you're Smokey's friend, and I know you've been married and I thought you could talk some sense into him. He's a good guy, really, it's just that he thinks he can play cowboy for the rest of his life and doesn't think about his family."

"Kitten," I said, "this is really between the two of you and I don't think I . . ."

"But he'll *listen* to you, Buck," she said. "He has to listen to somebody. You see how it is, don't you? You have to see it."

There was an edge in her voice I'd never heard there before. Not from her, anyway.

"Most men want to take care of their families," she said, "but not him. He'd rather ride horses with his buddies and stay away all day and sometimes until late in the night. Do you know that during the gather he's gone for a week straight and we don't see him or hear from him at all?"

"Of course."

"And then he doesn't always come home, but he'll go to town and have a beer with his friends, and here we sit way out here, but he doesn't care."

"Look Kitten," I said as gently as I could. "He's a cowboy. That's what he does for a living. And he's good at it. He could get a job on any cow outfit or pack station in the country. And he's a hard worker, too. Being a cowboy sometimes means being gone for a week on a gather, or working late shipping cattle. You know that's how it's done, and you knew that before you married him."

"Sure," she said, and I didn't like the look I got. "Sure. It's just like you to make excuses for him. You're no better, Buck. You work in town, but you're just a damn cowboy like the rest of them."

I stood up and started for my hat.

"Go ahead, just walk out. That's the easy way, isn't it? That's the *cowboy* way. When something gets tough, just grab your hat and ride off."

"Well," I said, "I don't know what you want from me, Kitten. Honest to God I don't. I know you're unhappy, but I'm damned if I know what I can do about it. I'm sorry you two are having troubles, but I really don't see..."

"He'll listen to you, Buck," she said. "You may be the only person in the world he'll listen to. If you'd just talk to him, I know he'd grow up and straighten out and see there are things we need."

"Like a washing machine?"

"And why not? And moving to town, too. Is that too much to ask? There are men in town who work out on the ranches and come home at night. I'm not asking him to move to L.A. or anything. Just to town. You know there isn't a kid Crystal's age to play with for about thirty-five miles? How's she going to have any fun?"

"She sure *seems* happy . . ."

"Well, I mean how is she going to learn to play with other children? To learn things?"

She was quiet for a minute and just looked at me, standing by the hat rack.

"You're not going to do it, are you?"

"What's that?"

"Talk to him! You're not going to talk to him, are you?"

"No. I'm not."

"You're just like he is, aren't you?"

I thought about that for a minute, too.

"Maybe I am, Kitten. We're different in many ways, but we're alike in some ways, too. Maybe I agree with him that this is a good life and a good way to raise a child. Maybe *I'd* be inclined to move to town so my child would have other children to play with, but I can't see anything wrong with this right here, since you're asking. And there's one more thing, too. Smokey is the closest friend I've ever had, and the quickest way to lose that friendship is to meddle in his family life, and that's the reason I'm going to stay out of it."

She looked at me and smiled slowly, raising an eyebrow, and I knew then what she'd look like when she was fifty years old.

"You're going to stay out," she said, in a measured voice, "even if it means he loses his wife and child?"

"Yes," I said. "Even if it means that. Look, I'm sorry about this, but you two have to work these things out for yourselves."

Then I grabbed my hat and scooped up my bedroll from the couch and backed into the screen door to leave. But I stopped for a minute. I looked at her face. I'd seen that face before, but not on her.

"Kitten, tell me one thing before I go. Let's say Smokey quits his job and goes to town and he becomes whatever it is you want him to become. Let's just say that he does all that, okay? How long would you stay with him?"

She glared at me.

"Be honest," I said. "Just between us. You'd leave anyway, wouldn't you? You're going to go anyway, aren't you?"

"Damn you Buck."

"Kiss the baby for me," I said. I heard the tears start before the screen door clicked behind me.

Chapter Sixteen

WE BOTH LAY AWAKE A LOT THAT NIGHT in that little camp by the waterfall. Talked some and wondered what would happen when the sun came up. It was a good night, with a big moon, and it made the rough hills ricochet shadows like some other world, a planet where there was no noise, no sound except for the soft chuckles of the waterfall and the occasional pop of the sage wood in the fire. And there was nothing there but Chuckles and Duster and Smokey and Buck and a thousand hills with a thousand, maybe three thousand, horses.

A magic time, and I spent what minutes I could thinking of Jan and trying to see her face clearly. She smiled at me, like always, but there was something distant in the smile now, some pain that wasn't there before. Something had tempered the smile, and I knew what it was, and I knew who had done it, and the shame and the blame came back to me and then I knew things. And they weren't good. And when my eyes closed, it was the dark-haired girl who was smiling, and there was no reserve in her smile. And I enjoyed it and hated myself.

Somewhere along the way we dozed off, and it was still dark when Smokey kicked the fire back to life and the sparks went flying up to their creator and the horses nickered for the grain in their *morals*. They stomped impatiently, as an animal will when it is in top shape and wants to run.

All through coffee and some bacon and bread, there was no talking between us. It could be we were all talked out, but it was more than that, because it was a morning where words were almost sacrilegious. A simple "good morning" could sound profane.

We checked the horses' shoes quietly by flashlight, and then the awesome quiet of the morning was cracked by Smokey tightening the clinches on one of Duster's hind shoes.

We saddled up and carefully felt the spread of the blankets so no folds or creases could set a sore on the horses, and we felt the skirts of the saddles to make certain they sat down even. We checked chin straps and latigos and headstalls for pinches. We tied extra ropes on behind the cantleboards with saddle strings, hung our best nylon catch ropes on the horses and tied them hard and fast.

Smokey bent his knees and stretched, the way we did before a contest ride. I swung my arms around and swiveled back and forth to loosen up, then kicked dirt in the fire.

Then it was quiet and we saw each other only as silhouettes, and we felt the little desert morning chill that tantalizes humans during hot weather. We both swung up at the same time, then reached across and shook hands.

"Which do you want?" he asked. "The ridge by Cow Spring or the round spring?"

"I'll take Cow Spring, if that's okay with you."

"You don't mind splitting up like this?"

"Seems right," I said. "It's an alone kind of a job, isn't it?"

"Some things are."

"Some things," I agreed.

The horses were stamping anxiously now, and Duster started flipping his head in anticipation.

"Think you can keep a leg on each side and your mind in the middle?" Smokey said.

"You think that roan horse can find his way to the catch pen about noon after you fall off?"

I could feel the grin on his face.

"Like the old-timer said, Buck, you just go out and find a horse and then bring him back."

"Simple."

"Simple."

"Nothing to it."

"Let's catch wild horses," he said.

Duster walked up with a head-shaking impatience to the little ridge behind the falls, and Smokey waved once as they were sky-lined along the long ridge toward the round spring.

I turned Chuckles's head to the east and his powerful hindquarters took us to the top of the little ridge in three hunches, and we set off at an easy trot toward the pink glow of morning.

The music came then, sifting upward from the black earth of predawn, climbing like fog wisps and sitting gently on the ears of the mind. The music of morning and solitude. I recall thinking that Ravel's *Daphnis and Chloe* should never be heard in a concert hall, or while people are leaping about in tights, but out here when the east starts to pink up. It should be heard with the song of the raven and the meadowlark and the whuffing of the horses as they walk briskly and their breath makes little clouds that float back and taste of barley.

The music came with the dawn and grew with the light and then it was day, those few minutes later. Then came the warm morning smell, and my arms thawed out, and that good bay horse Chuckles began his

Coso mustang radar. His ears worked as we rode along, first this way and then the other. He was a good horse and he knew what he was to do. You showed him the direction to take, and he'd look for horses.

We dropped down off the first ridge and crossed a sagebrush flat separating it from the next ridge. I was swinging a loop by this time, trying to remember which size is best for horses. A cowboy today almost never has occasion to rope a horse. The subject doesn't arise. I tried various loops and finally settled for something about the size of a head loop in team roping, with plenty of leader in it for stiffening. This warmed me up, and swinging it was good, and then I saw how hard Chuckles was working, so I just hinted with the spurs and he relaxed into a good controlled lope, radar working hard, and we sailed across that sagebrush flat easily, like ballet dancers.

He hunched on to the top of the next ridge, and we started down it into the secret heart of the Cosos, that badland of lava and chunks and cliffs and the rare seeps that mean home to the wildest horses in the nation. On some days this area could be forbidding, and on others it could take on the air of a bad joke played on someone else.

The tracks of a large bunch of unshod horses were beneath our own shod hooves then, and Chuckles raised his head higher, ears still working. We started up an arroyo and then Chuckles stopped, quivering, his head up and his ears slammed forward into a point.

I slipped down and took several deep knee bends to loosen up, then buckled hobbles on Chuckles and tied the reins to the connecting strap. I took off the chaps, put a sneak on the lip of the next rise, and peeked over.

There they were.

Hundreds of wild horses in the sage-dotted valley were before me, mostly bays and blacks with some buckskins sprinkled through the herd like salt. I lay still and watched them move, these horses that had never felt a rope. They grazed, and then looked up and around, so the herd looked like a symphony of bobbing heads.

The herd was actually a number of herds, each subgroup with its own stallion and lead mare. The lead mare always picked out the deepest choicest grass, kicking any who challenged her. The stallion circled his portion of the mares and babies, looking threateningly at anyone who came close.

This was repeated time and again across this valley between hills of swelling yellow dirt and black killer rocks. Always the same. A little dance of vigilance, if you will. Freedom has its price. And there was a symmetry, a balance to it.

The nearest horses were maybe two hundred yards in front of me and the wind was right in my face, so this was the best approach. From the time we topped this ridge, it would be only seconds before the horses were in flight. I looked down the hill at Chuckles and saw him at full alert, but quiet and still. A nervous pawing this far away would be enough to send a stallion to investigate, or maybe they would just all panic and quit the country. When it comes to a good first-cabin panic, horses wrote the book. The hobbles were a good idea.

At this distance, there may be some horsemen who can pick out a good horse, a sound horse, or a young horse. That is what I wanted, of course. But there's no way I could pick one out at two hundred yards. Oh, maybe if one were missing a leg, I could see him limp from that far away and scratch him off the list, but that would be about it. So I lay there, in no hurry to break this pastoral scene into its component parts of violent hooves and snaking rope.

I realize there are big herds of wild horses running loose all over the West right now, but it's hard to ignore reality. The handwriting is on the wall for wild horses. Yes, they are protected now, but only from people who would catch and use them. They are prey to crowding, disease, starvation, and death. They are protected from the mustangers now, but that will have to change. I'm afraid I have no faith in the common sense of any governmental group. It's as though there is an equation saying the more minds put to solving a problem, the less common sense the answer will have. If Congress made a mistake by not allowing anyone at all to catch wild horses, it will more than likely try to rectify that by wiping them all out. But even if lightning were to strike the funny building with the round roof, and a compromise was found, the horses were likely to come out short, anyway. Horses like land and grass and water. So do people.

That might be of some use as an epitaph for these animals someday.

So I lay there and just watched them. Lay there until I could feel every pebble beneath me, digging into my skin. Lay there until my arms went to sleep. And as I watched them, I thought of the refrain hunters of the north country secretly said to themselves high on a tundra ridge just before making a final stalk on the ocean of palmated antlers that was a migrating herd of caribou—"I wonder which of you grazing peacefully right now will have his life change drastically in the next few minutes. Your life will change and so will mine, but only I can decide that."

I looked back down the hill at my horse, quivering his sleek muscles beneath his new, slick summer coat. He was in shape. I was in shape. We came here to do a job, and by smash, let's go rope a wild horse.

It took only a small tightening to bring the cinches up snug. I buckled on the chaps and checked the horn knot on the catch rope. Snug and tight. A glance showed all four shoes were on and ready.

This was it. Checked everything. When we topped that rise, I wanted to be in overdrive. I stepped aboard, built a loop in the nylon catch rope, and ran my hand along the back of Chuckles's neck just to be friendly. Then I touched him with those rowels and we hopped over the ridge and shot down into the tailings of that panicked herd like demons.

Necks were bobbing, like fish spawning upstream, but there was a sea of necks, with forelocks and manes flying, and tails, and some broke off to the left and to the right, and we let them go. The old stuff and the very young broke off and went around, but the necks ahead of us now, fifty yards ahead of us, were in for the fight. They were in for the chase, and so were we.

Chuckles scattered gravel so smoothly that I just kept the tail of the loop tucked beneath my armpit and watched around me at the multi-colored sea through which we sailed so effortlessly.

Then there were two ahead, flying, seeming to fly, floating along through the sage like pounding ghosts. A sorrel and a buckskin. Both clean-limbed and floating, flying in this old, old dance. And it was our turn to dance it with him. Thank you. The buckskin took my fancy, so when the two separated, I nudged Chuckles's head toward the buckskin, and the sorrel flaked off and back like a jet fighter peeling out of formation.

And then it was us and the buckskin. I yelled, "Hello!" at this horse, then gave an "Eeeeeeha!" and leaned forward as if I could help Chuckles along. And the buckskin we chased in this old sweet dance was a banshee devil of the mountains, diving into arroyos, charging into lava beds, and then opening new bursts of speed out on the flats. But at last it was a long flat before us, reaching off to the south, this one, and we'd have a long run and a good run, and this was what we'd waited for, because the yards between us diminished as though in slow motion. Forty, then thirty, then twenty.

The weeks of grain for Chuckles and the running and conditioning were paying off. The inborn speed he got from his father had evened things up between a riderless wild animal and this two-part unit of ours that was trying to work.

And then the bobbing neck was there, and I felt Chuckles throw an extra spurt into it. He knew his business and this was it. And then the loop was up and was swinging and I threw.

The loop flopped alongside the horse's neck and quickly slid off. I built another loop as Chuckles continued to rate this wild horse ahead of us. And the loop was now ready and came up for a swing, and somehow I knew this time. Then through the morning music of the mountains and the violence of our little dance here in front of God, I could hear the words of Ross, so many years ago when I missed a calf.

"You soft-looped him," he'd said. "You throw that rope like an old lady, you'll never catch anything."

So I did as I was told and concentrated on that spot just behind the ears where the little bump lived, and I swung that rope and Chuckles laid his ears back a bit tighter, and then I stared a burning tunnel through that little bump by the horse's ears and threw that loop the way I'd pitch a baseball at that one little spot.

The loop whipped out, the honda touching that bump. Then the loop flared out around, dropped over the horse's head, and I grabbed the rope and pulled the slack taut.

Chuckles sat down hard in the sagebrush, but this wasn't some calf to be flipped, but a nine hundred-pound horse, so I just had time to say oh-dear-Jesus when all hell hit the end of that rope and all three of us went down.

Looking back on it now, I still don't know how that horse managed to stay beneath me. Before I had time to bail out, some sagebrush whipped my face and then we were up again, and I was still in the saddle, and we were back in business and securely tied to a screaming wild animal trying to fling his various parts to the four corners of the earth.

For the first time, as we dodged and danced and faced this dervish, I saw we'd roped ourselves a young stud horse.

He screamed and plunged, then fell and got up and plunged and screamed, then made one run for us, but changed his mind before he got there and shot off to the left and damn near jerked us down again when he came to the end of that thirty feet of nylon catch rope.

And there was old Chuckles, just working rope like we were in an arena with the stopwatch on us. We were both sweating, and the little mustang was sweating, and it was a bit like tying onto a large grayling with a two-pound tippet on the fly rod. We'd give a little, then back up and take a little, and that buckskin was giving it holy bananas with all four feet. No quit in this rascal, I thought. He'd be a good horse. He'd do, for sure.

But he finally just lay back against that rope, made choking sounds, and toppled over. I untied one length of rope I had behind the cantle and stepped off Chuckles to go down and claim our horse. Chuckles kept the rope just taut, and I ran down and tied a large bowline around the horse's neck, then flipped a loop of rope around one hind pastern and drew it up toward the loop and tied it off. He wouldn't be moving too fast in that foot rope.

I grabbed the loop around the horse's neck and gave a quick jerk to loosen it enough to let some more air in, and that buckskin sucker jumped up and reached for me with those teeth while I was making it back to the saddle in record time.

Well, the foot rope and my smell so close to his nostrils gave the little guy another dose of the fighting fantods, and he went to it again. The foot rope made him panic some more, and he did his grunts and flips and strikes the best he could. Then he went down again.

This time I slipped off my Levi jacket and pulled it over his face, tying the sleeves under his throatlatch to blindfold him. He lay stretched out and quivering. The fight was done. When that blind comes down and the lights go out, the toughest horse in the world shuts 'er down.

I took down some more rope and fixed a rope halter on him, then ran the catch rope through it and through the neck rope and fixed it fast around his girth. When this was done, I snapped the catch rope at Chuckles and backed him into the slack, then eased my jacket off the mustang's face and trotted back to the saddle. But this time he lay there and breathed hard and looked at us.

So I talked to him, and Chuckles did, too, in a way. We just sat there, this unlikely trio in the middle of a desert mountain range, and we told him things weren't that bad. And while I spoke, I looked down at this sleek wild animal with my ropes all over him. He looked kind of pitiful, trussed up that way, but if you looked in his eyes and tried to think like he did, he looked kind of cute, too. I began to like him.

When his breathing became regular again, he lurched to his feet, making it on the third try. He looked at everything and sniffed everything and twitched around a lot, but mostly he just looked at us standing there talking to him.

It was still morning, and there was no panic for time, so I thought we'd just try and talk him gentle. I believe it worked, too.

I just explained to him that being wild wasn't such a good idea for a horse, because there weren't any guarantees on feed that way. And being a stud horse out there in the Cosos? Hey, you could find better deals than that. If you weren't the biggest and toughest and rankest stud horse on the mountain, you were going to be off living a pretty lonely life with some other bachelors. And let's say you *were* the rankest old bronc in the country. What that brought you was a life of scars and bruises and tooth marks just from trying to hold onto what was yours. It was not fun, mustang, remember that. Wouldn't it be nice to just take a day or two off in some green pasture and play around with your pals? Fun stuff. Horse stuff. Why, there'd be some flesh on your young tough bones, my friend.

And he listened, I think. He stood there watching us, his head stretched out toward us as he drank in the wind from our sweaty bodies. And he swirled the new smells around in his big black nostrils and tasted every nuance of scent, setting it in his mind. He shook his head, then stretched out for more scent. Twice he fell back against the rope, but that was all, because with the elaborate rig I had on him, sometimes called a "cowboy's come-along," when he hit the end of that rope, it squeezed him around the girth and shot him forward, and with the rope run through his makeshift halter, he was forced to face us.

For more than an hour old Chuckles and I had a visit with this wild horse. He was still plenty alert, but that look of panic wasn't there anymore.

Years back a wonderful professional roper told me the only thing dumber than a horse was an earthworm, but not everyone agreed with him. One cowboy who was there said that was unkind to earthworms, and put the intelligence quotient of a horse flapping senselessly somewhere between that of today's domesticated turkey and a flat brown rock.

Because a horse is not, in fact, an intellectual prairie fire, it takes a little longer for some things to sink in. Like capture. We sat there talking to this buckskin for a long time and finally you could see the acceptance in his eyes. Yes, mustangs are wild, but only until you show them they aren't anymore. I've always believed in keeping total control of the situation, then go one step at a time, and give the old pony time to get used to each step. My theory is that horses would learn more quickly if the trainers would just go off and read a book for an hour each time they introduced something new.

Finally I stepped down and started down the rope to the mustang. This took maybe ten minutes, talking softly all the time. To a horse, ten minutes is a short time. By the time I reached for his neck and touched him, he was ready enough for me that he just stood there and quivered but took it. After all, he was still alive, and I hadn't done any of the things necessary to kill him or eat him, which is what he expected from this situation. I rubbed his neck and withers and talked to him a lot more, and while he didn't like it, he decided to tolerate it. It takes time for those messages to sink in through layers of bone and gristle, but once they register, it seems to be all right.

I talked to this horse and petted him until he was quiet and as content as a horse is able to be when he's lashed up like Joan of Arc at a barbecue. Then I went way around him and approached him from the other side. Naturally, he acted as though he'd never seen me before, so we had to start all over again getting acquainted on the other side. Horses are like that. We got to the neck petting part and talking until both sides of this bronc were petting proof.

He began to relax, and I slipped my jacket over his head again. He made one jump, but then lay back against the rope and stopped while I tied the sleeves to blindfold him. Then I took off the foot rope, letting his hind leg down to the ground, walked back to Chuckles, and tied that foot rope behind the cantle where I'd gotten it. I rode Chuckles slowly up to the wild horse, who quivered and blew as he smelled Chuckles approaching but was frozen in his tracks by the blindfold.

We talked to him another ten minutes, maybe, then I reached down and pulled off the jacket.

And he stood there, two feet away, just looking at us.

I reached over and touched him on the neck, and rubbed that a little, telling him it was going to be all right, then I turned Chuckles toward the catch pen down in the canyon and rode away. When the rope tightened, the mustang fought it, then came up a little. Then we started off and he fought it again, and we waited until he was through and had time to cool off, then we started again.

He began taking a step or two toward us, then we'd ride a step or two ahead and take the slack out of the rope. He'd walk forward, and we'd walk forward. In another thirty minutes, he'd figured out how this was supposed to work and figured out we weren't there to hurt him. He followed us down the canyon and across the flat, and two hours later I led him into the catch pen and closed the gate.

Just before dark, I heard a war whoop on the ridge above us and Smokey and Duster rode down, leading one of the prettiest blaze-faced sorrel mares I'd ever seen.

"What do you think, pard?" he yelled. "Think ol' Grant will settle for this one?"

"Hell, I think the shock will kill him," I said, grinning big as life as he rode in the corral and tied up his stock.

"Nice little buckskin," he said, like we did this every day. "Stud horse? Can't see too well."

"Yeah, a little stud."

"Give you much fight?"

"Some, but not too bad. I'm not missing any fingers or ears."

"I guess I made up for it," Smokey said. "Which I guess is only right since I'm not the city boy of this outfit. Amigo . . . partner . . . let me introduce you to the witch of the West. You see this pretty little sorrel mare? She is a kicking, striking she-devil and I guarantee I did some old stud horse a favor by removing her from his harem. Goldang, Buck, she had me down twice, and if it weren't for my old partner Duster, here, she'd have eaten me for sure."

He grinned.

"And run? I jumped this little bunch she was with right before noon. I could've roped one of the others, but that would have been the smart thing to do. Oh hell no. I see this pretty little mama shooting down this canyon and all I can think of is I've found Grant's mare. I mean, it isn't his mare, of course, but it could be her granddaughter or something, couldn't it?"

I looked at the mare and nodded. She fit the description pretty closely.

"So I'm thinking to myself how happy it'll make the old man when he sees this mare, and I let all them other *good* horses go and take off after her. Hey, pard, this bitch could win the Kentucky Derby. I musta run her close on to ten miles before I got a loop on her, and you know old Duster here can run. Then, when I got her roped, all holy hell broke loose. Do you think she fights and chokes herself down like a good little wild horse should? Hell no. Not this angel of pain. This one hits the end of the rope, spins around, takes one look at us and screams, 'Lunch!'

"I'm not kidding, Buck. She tried to eat us both. She's a damn cannibal! But she wasn't going to eat us until we'd both been properly tenderized by her front hooves. What I mean, if old Duster here wasn't already a gelding, she'd have taken care of that and then started on me. I've about had a full day, amigo. I've been under Duster once and that mare twice and I can tell you I've seen better sights than looking up at the diamond on the belly part of Duster's cinch. A man shouldn't be in a place like that. Hell, look at my shirt. I'm all eat up. I'm done in and finished for good and I doubt if I survive the night. But if I do . . . I'm going to ride that bitch in the morning."

I just looked up at him and grinned. "Well, they say fresh air and sunshine are good for a guy."

"Shut up," said Smokey.

"Why?"

"Talkin' draws lightning."

Then we both grinned and shook hands.

"Hot damn, city boy, we done 'er, didn't we?"

"Slicker'n chrome on a new trailer hitch."

"EEEEEEeeeeee- HAAAAaaaaa!"

"Me, TOOOOooooooo!" I yelled, and then we both sat down by the little fire I'd built and just stewed in our own honest sweat and smiled.

"By golly, Buck, are you too tired to do anything right now?"

"Smoke, I'm too tired to breathe. In fact, I'm not breathing. It's my shirt. It got in the habit of going in and out, in and out, and the sucker just pushes air in and out like an iron lung."

"Look, come help me for a minute, Buck. Just a minute while we still have light enough to see."

Smokey went to his saddlebags and came back with a loose cinch ring. He threw it on the coals of the fire and sat back down.

"A running iron?" I asked.

"Tomorrow I'm going to ride that sorrel Jezebel and turn her into a United States citizen, so let's brand her tonight and get that part over with."

"Brand her?"

"Yeah," he looked at me and smiled, "with the Slash G. What do you think?"

The Slash G . . . Grant's brand. I don't know that anything more than the horse he rode ever carried it, but that was *his* brand. Most cowboys had one registered somewhere or other, even if they never used it. It was mostly dream stuff . . . it was for thinking of all the fat cattle that would someday wear that brand in belly-tall grass.

"By God, Smoke, every once in a while you make sense. You think that thing's hot enough?"

"Will be by the time we waltz old Matilda to the ground. You ready?"

Slim Randles - 129

"I was born ready."

"Let's do it."

In a few minutes, we had fixed leg ropes on the mare and laid her gently down. Not that she went through any of this gently. She pawed at the moon, even when her hind legs were immobilized, but finally she was hogtied and fairly still and the three of us had gotten to this point without any maiming injuries.

Smokey found two green sage sticks and stuck them through each way on the cinch ring in the time-honored method of the rustler, then gripped the ends. The glow of the ring showed well as he approached. It was that dark by then.

I sat on the sorrel's head and grabbed the foot ropes tightly as the iron touched the hide on her left shoulder and the acrid smell of burning hair stung our nostrils. She squealed and strained at the ropes as Smokey did his artistry on her skin. In a few seconds, it was done, and there was at least a recognizable Slash G on her shoulder.

Smokey threw the cinch ring into the sand outside the pen and ran her lead rope through the fence, taking a dally around a good stout post. Then he stood there on the outside of the corral looking at me with this mare's head in my lap and he says kinda easy like, "Okay, Buck, now just e-e-ease them foot ropes off her and run like billy hell."

"Thanks a lot, friend," I said. "You remember how to get to my house?"

"I don't know. Maybe. Why?"

"For the reading of the will. Oh hell, here goes."

I slipped the ropes off, released her head, and rolled backwards in the same motion while I heard the singing of the slack through the fence as Smokey tightened his dallies, and I was moving as quickly as I could. One hoof narrowly missed ending my family line, and I felt something tug at me from behind. Then I was clear and the mare was snubbed back up to the post. We had all survived it.

"Lordy, can you pick 'em!" I said. "That's a man-eating she-cat from the Cosos. Hell, Smoke, why didn't you rope a goddanged mountain lion? I hear they're at least good eating."

Smokey was laughing now and pointing at my butt. I turned around and looked and half my back pocket was ripped loose, my billfold on the verge of falling out. I took it out and it felt wet, so I went over to the fire and looked at it. That was horse slobber on the leather, along with unmistakable tooth marks.

"The bitch tried to eat me!"

"Old son, you shoulda seen you! I about died laughing. I thought she'd nipped half your ass off with that bite. Shoulda seen you move! If I'd known you had that much action, I'd have put you in the follies."

We hunkered by the fire on the warm spring night, listening to our horses in the corral, both wild and domestic, and smelling dust and manure and the salt grass over by the little brackish spring. It was a real good feeling.

We unsaddled Chuckles and Duster and left them tied near the mustangs to quiet them, then cut grass for all four of them and hauled water to them in our hats. The mustangs would not touch either the grass or the water, but we knew they would in the morning. Chuckles and Duster settled down and rested as we rubbed their backs with grass and brush. I touched the buckskin on the neck and talked with him a few minutes, but Smokey wasn't about to get near either end of that sorrel mare.

Then we took off our chaps and spurs and just sat by the fire and kept it going. It was something to do. We knew we wouldn't be eating tonight because neither of us brought food from camp, neither of us were about to go get it, and we were both too tired to eat it, anyway.

Tired, and maybe just a little excited, too.

"Damn!" Smokey said slowly, grinning and shaking his head.

"We did it, pard."

"Middle-aged hell," he said. "I'm young and tough and incredibly good looking..."

"Don't forget modest as hell..."

"Damn right! That's one of my more outstanding virtues. Kiss my butt, world! You are looking at two mustanging sonsabitches from the high country!"

"Cut your throats in envy!" I yelled.

"And you know what else, world?" he shouted. "Tomorrow I'm not going to be able to walk. Christ! I think I'm hurt bad."

"Well, the lungs seem to work all right, Smoke."

"Yeah, but I think I put a permanent kink in something that shouldn't be bent that way."

"Well," I said, "I was all right until you sicced that sorrel alligator on me. Damn! I've known war dogs that were friendlier'n that. Compared to her, it'd be fun kissing a meter maid on the mouth!"

"Quality, my friend," Smokey said. "Pure quality. Don't you know it's always the horses you have the most trouble with that you end up being the proudest of?"

"The hell you say."

"Fact. I swear it."

"The ones you have the most trouble with are the ones you end up..."

"Being the proudest of, yes sir. That's a fact, too."

"Smokey, this sorrel wolverine you tied into must be destined to win the Olympics, the Triple Crown, and the damn Nobel Prize for science."

"Yeah," he grinned, "unless she kills the judges first."

It was so good, with the warm night breeze sifting down through the sage to us, and the burgundy smell of the sage fire making up for empty bellies.

We sat a long time without talking, then stretched out on saddle pads with our heads on the saddle skirts and grinned at each other across the fire.

"It feels good to just sit," I said.

"Know what you mean," he said. "It feels good to do something physical like this, and at the end of the day you can look at it and actually *see* what you've done. Now, would you say this is the best thing you've done in ages, Buck? Would you admit that this beats sitting in an office and listening to horns honk?"

"Yes," I said. "Yes. This kind of life, with all its bumps and stinks and warts, is better."

"Would you say, ol' Buckaroo, that this is the grandest thing a man can do?"

And he ducked and laughed as I chucked a rock in his direction, but I was laughing too hard to be very accurate.

He looked at me and smiled. "Well, hell, goddang . . ."

" . . . I mean to say," I added.

" . . . the way it was . . ."

I laughed. "Now you take in there . . ."

"That pain?" Smokey said. "Oh God, I've got to get some sleep. You know how bad I'm gonna hurt in the morning? Hell, I already feel like a sick dog threw me up."

"I knew you reminded me of something, Smoke, but I couldn't think of what it was."

Then it was my turn to duck.

The fire was down to just a good glow, and I lay there and listened to the snuffling of the four horses over there in the corral. The poles on the corral were that flickering bone color in the firelight, while the world beyond them lay cradled in that mystery that comes with a still night. Soon I heard Smokey's even breathing and knew I should be asleep, too, but instead, I stuck a few more sage roots on the coals and quietly blew them into young flames. It wasn't going to be easy to sleep tonight.

I looked around and there was my pard and the corrals and the horses and the night, with the waning moon just rising over the secrecy of the Panamint Mountains, and up above were the sharp stars of a desert night. How many nights had I spent like this, looking up into a swarming heaven and thinking?

And that night I smiled and said quietly to the heavens, here I am again, friends, a little older and a bit more stove up tonight, but in some ways a lot younger than I was a month ago. And tonight I know, friends, that I have to find a way to feel this good more often. And I will. The night is too sweet to ever waste again.

There have been so many nights. Some good and sweet like this one, and there have been some bad ones, too.

Then there are those nights that don't seem to fit either classification strongly. Good and bad seem to tug at them for supremacy, but what usually wins the contest is being memorable. For things happen on those nights that change forever the way a man thinks, about himself and about his best friend.

It was a quiet time, and I usually reserved these times for thoughts about Jan, but tonight was different. Tonight about all I got was a feeling of comfort and warmth and love about Jan, but then, in a few minutes, I kept coming back to her voice on the phone, her voice asking me if I were still going, the hurt in her eyes. If only we'd been married a year . . . but that record was getting old and worn out and kept sticking in the same place. I knew a man had to do what must be done. I knew that. But how does he really know what must be done? That was the question that kept coming back. Because everything I felt right then told me I was doing the right thing. Everything but the look on Jan's face, and now her features were blurring a bit around the edges, and I hated myself for letting that happen. An answer, I needed an answer. I was a good guy who wanted to be happy and to make a woman happy, too. So, should I become what she wanted me to be, or should I be complete, what I wanted to be, and then I'd be more attractive because I was happy? I'd seen men do it both ways. The ones who worked to fit their wife's idea of what they should be generally lasted a little longer, but was it really living? Sometimes they lasted a lifetime together, but was it the best thing to do?

The ones who went their own path seemed happier, but they were often alone. And there was the problem. There was the thing that wouldn't let us fall asleep easily each evening. Why couldn't a guy have it both ways? It was a problem of the night and the quiet hours, and I didn't believe there was an easy night answer, either.

This was another night in a necklace of nights that made up life, and strangely enough, after such a day as this, I found myself drawn back in time some fifteen years to one of those nights.

A night of memories and pain.

Chapter Seventeen

I WAS LIVING OUT in the southern Mojave Desert in those days, close to where it is stopped by the San Gabriel Mountains. Smokey, naturally, didn't call, but just drove into the yard where I was staying and announced I was going up to the Owens Valley with him. My college schedule was pretty open that year—and it wouldn't have mattered if it wasn't, anyway—so I just threw a bedroll in his pickup and we took off.

On that trip, it was his turn to be silent. I'll bet he didn't say ten words before we stopped at Reno's in Mojave for dinner, some thirty miles up the road. It was cold and overcast that day, I recall, with the clouds making a ceiling above the desert and hushing all below. It made the desert a cozier place and a friendlier place. People smiled at each other more on the big, straight highway through the Joshua trees. And it was very cold.

Reno's always looked like a comfortable, clean outdoorsman's whorehouse with good food. There were caribou and moose hanging from the red-flocked wallpaper and a collection of antique cameras. Every cowboy in the Owens Valley stopped there for at least coffee on every trip.

When the warmth of the place had a chance to sink through the clothes and touch the body, I asked Smokey where he'd been living.

"Down below," he said.

"What?"

"L.A."

I looked over at him. "You're kidding, right?"

He just shook his head and was quiet.

"L.A.?"

He nodded again.

"Why?"

"Doesn't matter now. Nothing matters now. It's all done."

"What's all done?"

"She got married."

"I'm sorry. I didn't know."

"She called me up to let me know. I always thought there was a chance, Buck. I mean, there's Crissie, so I thought maybe . . . oh hell."

"Yeah," I said.

He shrugged his shoulders and grinned a little hurt kind of grin.

"What you been doing, Buck, besides going to school?"

"That's about it, really."

"Know what you want to do yet?"

"Hell no."

"So why are you going to school?"

"Beats me. Lots of girls there, though." I grinned at him. We ate food and washed it down with coffee, and it was dark in Mojave when we got back in the pickup truck and started north again. I drove this time, and Smokey just sat there looking ahead, as though he could make the night slide by faster.

By the time we reached the Walker Pass junction, the snow began to fall. It came slowly at first, hesitatingly. Then it thickened up once it decided what to do and snowed in earnest.

The cars on the road became fewer and fewer, and you couldn't see the white line by the time we passed Little Lake.

"Looks serious," he said.

"I think it'll snow all night."

"You ever been to Sam's place in Haiwee Canyon?"

"Once or twice."

"I don't think Sam'd mind if we holed up in his bunkhouse tonight."

"Sounds good," I said.

I found the turnoff, and it was a squirrelly slide up to the bunkhouse by the corrals. This part of the desert was a pack station only in summer. I turned the truck around and headed her downhill before stopping, and we went in and made ourselves at home.

Smokey built a fire and found the makings for coffee while I dusted snow off our bedrolls outside and brought them in.

"Ever seen weather like this?" Smokey asked.

"Colder'n a witch out there."

"Won't be bad when this stove heats up," Smokey said. "Come on now, fire. Git a goin.'"

With the light of the kerosene lamp making the bunkhouse look soft, we took down a couple of mattresses hanging from the rafters and made our bunks and unrolled the bedrolls to let them warm up and found some chairs that worked pretty well to sit on when the fire got a little warmer.

Then the heat started, and we both went through the pleasant ritual of shedding layers of winter clothes as the heat increased.

"I like a hot fire," Smokey said, looking over at me.

"Let that sucker roar," I agreed.

Then, with the stove top glowing and the coffee water boiling, we got down to long johns, hats, and boots and made coffee.

"Smokey," I said, "this is better than whatever comes in second. Looking around me, it is my considered opinion that lots of other people aren't here right now, sharing this fire and listening to the snow. Hey, man, this is great!"

He raised a cup of coffee toward me in salute, and I continued.

"I'm sure glad you stopped by to get me, but damned if I know why yet. Why, it was just this morning I was thinking of coming up to this country anyhow, and reveling in the snowy vistas, the untrammeled quiet of a mountain meadow, the unmistakable mating cry of the forlorn, but hot-blooded . . ."

"Somebody vaccinate you with a phonograph needle?" Smokey asked.

"Sorry. It was just kinda quiet and I thought I'd liven things up a bit."

"Oh hell," he said, "I don't care. Go ahead."

"Ain't the same now. Nope. Once I get to the unmistakable mating cry of the hot-blooded what's-his-face, any little interruption and the mood is gone. Pffft! Just like that. Gone. Can't get it back now. Not a chance. I'm sorry, but you'll just have to wait until the next time."

I got up and put some more wood in the cookstove. Those babies can really throw out the heat, but they have such a small firebox, they'll nickel-and-dime you all night long to keep them going.

"Want to tell me about it?"

He looked up from his cup of coffee and shrugged.

"Don't matter," he said. "She's married now." He looked at me. "Take a guess who she married?"

"Somebody I know? One of those Bishop packers?"

"No. But take a guess who she married."

"Some guy who works for her dad?"

"By God, you did get smart in college."

"Wasn't that hard a guess."

"No, it wasn't. You know, Buck, you think sometimes maybe that's a surefire thing for her to do, but you keep hoping maybe things will change. You know what I mean?"

"Yeah. I know. Doesn't seem to work that way, though, does it?" I said. "It seems like once they're gone, they flip some little switch somewhere that changes them from loving to hating, and it's the big adios forever."

He nodded. "That's it. That's just how it happens."

"I was hoping things would be different for the two of you. I really had hopes."

"It wasn't two months ago, Buck, when I called her to see how Crissie was, and she said she'd think about it, you know?"

"Think about coming back?"

"Yeah. And I didn't hear from her any different until she called to say she was married. She said I ought to be happy about it because now Crystal has a father. I told her, hell, *I'm* her father, and she says sure, but now there's a father who's at home. Can you beat that? She moves out of my house and then says she found someone who'll stay home? Aw, hell . . . I don't know."

"I guess it's been pretty tough," I said.

"Tough? You don't know. Nobody knows."

He looked at me. "What am I, stupid or something, Buck?"

"Hell no."

"No. I mean it. I must be born dumb to go through this crap, and for nothing. Some goddang store clerk is sleeping with my wife and telling my daughter he's her daddy. And what do I do? Oh, hell, I am supposed to be grown up about things. That's what she said. Grown up."

I looked out the window. It was still snowing. Sometimes it's easier to watch it snow than to think about other things. Amazing things, snowflakes. By themselves, they are nothing, but when a bunch of them get together, and under the proper conditions, you can have a blizzard or an avalanche, or you can . . .

"I'm supposed to just say gee whiz, girl, that's wonderful that you called me up here to let me know you don't care about me anymore and have given my kid to some stranger to raise," Smokey said. "Hell, I'm so happy I think I'll wet my pants. No, I better not wet my pants. That's not being grown up."

"Smokey, I really think some things aren't meant to be. I really do. I think there are some things that just aren't going to work no matter how hard you both try or you want to."

"You don't know, Buck," he said, looking down at the smoke he was rolling and shaking his head. Then he looked at me. "I tried it her way, you know."

"I thought she wanted to move to town."

"Sure. And she did. I came home one night and found a note at the trailer house. She was long gone. And I went to town and she wouldn't see me. I could talk to her on the phone, but she just kept saying when was I going to grow up and accept my responsibilities and move to town and be a decent husband. Buck, I swear to you I never did anything against that woman. Not ever. And I told her I wanted to see Crissie and she said her father would bring Crystal down to the coffee shop and I could visit with her there."

"Did he come down?"

"Oh, yeah. He came down and brought the baby and I sat and talked with her and gave her an ice cream, and Kitten's dad sat right across from me and just waited. In about an hour, he said it was time to leave, and they left together. She was holding his hand . . ."

Smokey bit his lip and sat quiet for a bit. Then he lit his cigarette and took a couple of puffs.

"And it was like that every time I went to town. They... well, it was like they was afraid I'd run off with her or something. Didn't trust me with my own daughter."

"I'm sorry."

"So was I. Sorry as hell. And I got to thinking what was important to me, you know? By this time I wasn't really thrilled with Kitten, but I wanted that little girl. So I thought maybe I'd try it her way. You know, give it a try and see if I could do 'er."

I looked at him and he looked older than I remembered.

"I didn't say nothing to Kitten about it. Hell, Buck, I was going to surprise her, but she surprised me with that new husband first."

"Was that what you were doing in L.A.?"

He nodded.

"Where were you down there?"

"Hell, I don't know. One of them damn cities. They all run together and look alike, so it don't matter much."

"Why in the hell were you down *there*?"

"I was in school, pard," he said, with a weak grin. "Me! In school! I went down there four months ago and signed up for carpenter school. You see those things they have on TV where you go learn from them for six months and they help you find a good-paying job afterwards? Well, I called them last spring and they told me how much it would cost and cripes I couldn't believe it! But I rode colts for this guy last summer in the morning and evening and still rode for the brand all day. Hell, I was riding colts out in this guy's arena with the lights on. Them poor little bastards probably think nobody will ride them when the sun's out.

"Well, I did it. I got it. All of it. I paid for the course, just barely, and

I went down there and I been living with these friends of mine for all this time. Four goddanged months. You know what it's like to live down there for four months? Oh yeah, I forgot."

"I know what you mean."

"It was awful," Smokey said. "I think it was the worst idea I've ever had, and I've had a pocketful of bummers, as you know."

Smoke got up to reload the stove. Sometimes it takes a guy a few minutes to do this, because in shuffling the wood around in the firebox, it lets a guy figure out just what to say next.

"There was this school, you know. That took all day. And then at night there ain't a single damn thing to do there. Not if you're broke. Sit and watch TV with my friends, that's it. They were really great. Hell, I was broke."

He lowered his voice to a whisper and looked straight at me.

"They had to buy my cigarettes, Buck. Nobody, not ever, had to buy *me* any cigarettes in my whole life. But they had to do it, and they never said a word against me and let me sleep on the couch and fed me."

Smokey walked over to the one window and looked out. It was still snowing.

"Still snowing," he said and sat down again.

"You know what that was like, Buck? I was so broke I couldn't even pay attention. Hell, I didn't have lunch at all for four months. Couldn't afford it. When we stopped for lunch at the carpenter's school, I'd just go for a walk. The other guys thought I was eating in a café."

He grinned and shook his head, staring into the flickering light from the cracks around the pot lids on the stove.

"But you know, Buck . . . and this sounds stupid, I know . . . but you see, it was okay. Hell, all of it. I couldn't stand nailing boards together, and I sure as hell didn't like being broke all the time, but I just kept thinking how surprised Kitten would be when I graduated. You see,

I figured to just build things on ranches, you know, sorta ease into it. At least for a while."

"But you quit?"

"When she called me up the other day and told me about Wilson, hell, that was it. I told the teachers they could shove them two by fours and I found some day work and picked up some getaway money."

"What's Wilson's first name?

"That *is* his first name, Buck. Hell of a deal, ain't it? It's Wilson something-or-other, I forget. All she talked about was Wilson this and Wilson that and Wilson said this and Wilson plans to do that, and Wilson has this nice house in Bishop, and Wilson gave Crystal a swing set for a wedding present, and didn't I think that was nice? Anyway, his name is Wilson. I'll bet five bucks he don't want to be called Will, either."

"He might be an all-right guy. To be fair, I mean."

Smokey looked at me. "His name is *Wilson*, for God's sakes!"

"I see your point. So you're going to see them?"

"To see Crissie," he said. "To see my girl. I couldn't give a rat's ass for the rest of them, and that includes Wilson."

"Well, that's a good idea," I said. "Why don't you just drop me off in Independence and you can pick me up there later?"

"You gotta come with me to Bishop, Buck."

"Really, Smoke, there are times when someone like me would just get in the way, and I really think you'd be better off if you just drop me off in Independence."

"I ever ask you for much?" he said, and I could read his face in the lamplight.

"Can't remember you ever asking me for anything."

"Well, I'm asking this time. Asking hard. You gotta come with me to see my little girl. Look, it's important, okay? Just say it's important to me."

"Well, okay," I said. "Sure. If you really want me to."

"Yes."

"Hey, I'll be there," I said, a bit puzzled.

Smokey looked relieved at that, and we reminisced a bit and rode a few broncs there over coffee, and I even got a laugh out of him once. It came when we'd turned in and had blown out the lamp. There was just that little stove flicker for light, and the reassuring crackle of the fire.

"Buck," he asked softly, "do you ever wonder whether women have any idea how bad they hurt a guy?"

"Sometimes I wonder, pard. There are times when it seems like open season on our feelings."

"They can make a guy turn into an awful fool sometimes," he said, quietly.

"Well, that may be true in some cases," I said, "but with you and Kitten, I figure you came out way ahead on this deal."

He sounded shocked. "Just how the hell you figure *that?*"

"For one thing," I said, "you don't have to sleep with a guy named Wilson."

"By Jesus, that's right!" he said, and it was nice to just hear some laughter coming from him for a change.

"I'll be just a minute," he said. "You wait here and I'll go find out where Wilson's big beautiful house is."

Smokey walked into the hardware store and I could see him talking for long minutes with Kitten's dad and they seemed to be disagreeing on something. Finally, Kitten's dad wrote something on a piece of paper for Smokey and accepted Smokey's hand for a shake. As Smokey came out the door, I noticed his former father-in-law picking up the telephone.

Wilson's house was one of those good, stout Depression-era beauties that began cheap and became charming after about thirty years of use. From the looks of the well-trimmed hedge, I silently bet with myself that beneath that inch of snow, Wilson's lawn was edged. The walk was swept free of snow and standing on the walk at the curb, obviously waiting for us, was Kitten.

"Hi Kitten," Smokey said, although his voice shook just a little.

"You should've let me know you were coming," she said. "Wilson's down in Lone Pine today."

"Well, that's okay," he said. "I didn't come here to see old Wilson, anyway. I want to see Crissie."

"Her name is Crystal," Kitten said, "and you can see her right here. Not in the house. Right here. And listen, not for very long, either. Crystal is still very little and she gets confused these days. Is that all right with you?"

Smokey stood there on the curb and nodded. Kitten turned toward the house and waved, and a woman I vaguely remembered as Kitten's mother opened the screen door and let Crystal come running out into the yard in her heavy coat to hug her dad. Smokey stayed on his knees in the snow and held the little girl and whispered to her and brushed her hair back with his fingers and then he shook with sobs as he held her. Kitten watched a few minutes, then came over to the pickup.

"Hello, Buck," she said, in a friendly but reserved voice. "I'm glad he was able to get you to come. He didn't like it much, but I still think that's the best way to handle things. If you're here, I know you are level headed and will see everything's all right."

"You mean you told him..."

"That he could see Crystal sometime if you came along. Didn't he tell you?"

"Not in so many words, Kitten. Why did you do that? Has he ever tried to hurt you or Crystal?"

"Well, not yet, of course. But he *is* a cowboy, and Wilson says they're all alike."

I didn't want to get into this, so I just bit my lip.

"Wilson says we have to be careful what is said and done around Crystal right now, because she's impressionable. Wilson says the things she learns now she'll have for the rest of her life. That's why I wanted you here, Buck, so he'll be civilized when he visits her."

"Looks pretty civilized to me," I said, gesturing toward Smokey and Crystal, who were talking earnestly on the lawn.

"Wilson says men who live violent lives are violent toward others," she said, curtly. "Really, Buck, you went to *college*. You should know that."

"I must've been gone the day they discussed that, I guess."

Crystal came over to Kitten, dragging Smokey along by a finger.

"Mommy, I want to show Daddy my new room."

"No dear," she said, smiling. "Not today. You know your father said Smokey shouldn't go in our house unless he's home. Maybe some other time."

Smokey looked like he'd been bludgeoned.

"I'm her father," he whispered.

"What's that?" Kitten said.

"I'm her father," Smokey said. "*I'm* her father."

"Oh?" she said, smiling a sickly sweet kind of thing. "Are you really? What does a father do, Smokey? Does he go off playing or does he come home each day and take care of his family? Wilson says a father is as a father does."

"Look," Smokey said, "I'm Crystal's father. I'm *her* father."

"Well," Kitten said to Crystal, "I think this visit has lasted long enough. We'd better go back inside, dear. Smokey, if you want to visit again, you be sure to call first."

"What do you mean telling Crystal this Wilson guy is her father?" he said, his voice quavering. "She's *my* daughter."

"I was afraid this would happen. You see, Buck? Come along, Crystal. Let's go in."

Kitten took the little girl, who was crying by this time, and pulled her toward the house. Smokey started that direction but I caught him by the arm.

"Let go of me, goddammit! That's my daughter!"

"Sure it is, Smoke. Damn right. But let's go now, okay?"

"No. It sure as hell ain't *okay*," he said as the screen door opened and Kitten and Crystal disappeared inside. "She's my daughter, dammit!"

I grabbed his arm again and spun him to face me.

"Look," I said, as quietly as I could. "All you're going to do is screw things up so you'll never get to see her again. Get in the truck. Let's go for a drive and talk about it."

"Talk about it? That's all anybody does anymore. Talk about it. Dammit..."

He jerked free, spun around, and yelled. "You tell that goddamned Wilson sonofabitch that he can go straight to hell! Crystal's *my* daughter! Mine! And no two-bit..."

"Get in the damn truck!" I yelled, turning him away from the house. "Hell, Smoke, do you ever want to see your girl again?"

"I'll see her again, by God. I'll see her any damn time I want..."

"Not if you don't get in the damn truck and shut up," I said. "Why do you think her mother's here? A witness, Smoke. She's a witness who will tell the court that you threatened people and aren't fit to visit your daughter anymore. Can't you see what they want?"

He shut up, anyway, and just glared at the house.

"Yeah," he said. "I didn't think about that."

"Get in the damn truck."

"But I'm not going to just walk off and . . ."

"Yes you are, right now. Trust me. Do it."

I shoved him in the passenger side and slammed the door. I waved pleasantly toward the house and got in and drove the four blocks it took to get out of town and next to a pasture. He was raving all the way, and I stuck his keys in my pocket when we got out.

"What am I going to do?" he said, kicking a dead log and sending snow spraying from it. "What the hell am I supposed to do now? Some gunsil marries my wife and all of sudden he's Mr. God around here and I'm supposed to just forget my daughter and go off someplace. Right? Hell!"

"The way things are right now," I said, "you are Crystal's father and you have a right to see her. Reasonable visitation, they call it. That usually means whenever her mother thinks it's all right."

"What about when *I* think it's all right?"

I steered our little stroll through the light snow toward a stand of white-powdered locust trees over by a weir box.

"It isn't fair!" he said. "Where do they get off telling my daughter that this Wilson sonofabitch is . . ."

"Fair?" I said. "Who said anything about fair when you signed up with her? Nobody guarantees you a damn thing, pard. What you got to do is just accept that this isn't fair and say the hell with it."

"That's a bunch of bull," he said.

We were in the locust trees by this time and out of sight of the nearest houses.

"You know, Buck," he said, "I've got a good mind to set that little bitch straight on who the goddammed father is in this outfit! Did you see her smiling that little smart-ass smile at me? Like she's the Queen of England and I'm some dog turd she stepped on when she wasn't thinking straight. By God, I believe I'll go back there and have my two cents' worth out of that witch!"

He turned back toward the truck and I hit him as hard as I could on the side of the head. He staggered and almost went down.

"You dirty bastard!" he yelled. Then he was all over me. I took some good ones on the face and in the belly. I hit the snow after the third or maybe the fourth shot. It was hard to think clearly afterward about something like that. Of course, I had heavy clothes on and that helped some. Most of the time, I just tried to cover up and take it and listen to him calling me a dirty bitch and a rotten slut. I believe that was the first time I'd been called those names.

He went longer than I expected. Then it was over and he collapsed against the base of a big locust tree, sobbing. I dusted the snow off myself, wiped some of the blood off my mouth, and took inventory. All the parts seemed to be there and were functioning more or less as the owner's manual said they should, but they sure hurt like hell.

Two women down the street had come out of their houses to stare at us, and I gave them a friendly wave. They nodded and went back in.

I walked out away from the grove a ways to admire the care and craftsmanship that had gone into building this weir box, now softly covered with snow. I was still standing there making designs in the snow with the toe of my boot when I heard Smokey come up.

"You okay?" he asked.

I just grinned at him with a swollen mouth.

"Hey," he said, "I don't know what to say . . ."

"You got any of that getaway money left?"

"Yeah."

"Your turn to buy me dinner."

And when we finished eating and were having a smoke and looking out the window as Bishop dripped and puddled in the new sunshine, he said to me, "Why'd you do it?"

I looked over at him and shrugged. "I'm Crystal's Uncle Buck, remember? I think she's worth it."

He looked at me for a while, then smiled.

"I owe you one."

"Then answer one question for me, Smoke."

"Sure, anything."

I tried to look hurt. "Do you *really* think I'm a worthless whore?"

That wasn't really a high point in our lives, I thought, lying there in the mysterious Coso Mountains watching a friendly fire try to say hello to a waning desert moon. Not a high point, but it was something to remember.

Chapter Eighteen

I STUMBLED AROUND IN THE HALF-DARK and got the morning fire going and heard Smokey stirring in his saddle blanket. He was awake, but not very.

When the fire was up a good bit, I walked over in the morning light to look at our horses. The mustangs snorted a little but seemed content enough to stand there by the gentle stock. I brought each of them water in my hat, and this time they all took some, even the sorrel.

On my way back to the fire, where Smokey was starting to move, something under a sage caught my eye. I kicked at it and came up with a large tin can with about forty years of rust on it.

"Hey pard!" I yelled. "We're going to have some breakfast after all. I found a can."

"Found a can," he grumbled, pulling on his boots and cussing. "By hooters, that's just what I always wanted for breakfast, a tin can. Buck, don't you have any respect at all for a man who's been run over by a train or a dirty witch of a sorrel mare or anything?"

"Lordy, I haven't even had coffee and you're cheerful. I know there's a law against it somewhere."

I laughed at him as I scoured the can out with sand, then filled it half full of brackish water from the spring and adjusted some rocks for it on the fire.

"Now who's been vaccinated by that phonograph needle?" I chuckled.

"I still can't see what you're going to cook for us."

"Tea."

"Tea?"

"Yeah. Mormon tea or squaw tea. I've heard it called both. There's some right over here. Come on, I'll show you."

He grunted and groaned as he stumbled around the lip of the canyon to where the straight, grayish-green stems of the ephedra grew. I busted off a good handful and started back.

"We're going to eat those?"

"No, but we can brew some tea."

"Tea ain't breakfast, pard."

"You got a better plan?"

"No I don't."

"Well, try some of this. It's not the best there is in the world, but the old Indians swear by it. They got a name for it about this long. Two of the old Paiute ladies at the fort used to ask me to pick some for them on the sandhill on Sawmill Pass. There's a bunch of it up there. They said it helped their arthritis and they could go dance all night."

"Arthritis, huh?" he said, watching me crumble the green stems into the boiling water. "Wonder if it works on regular cowboy stove-ups."

"Only one way to find out."

"Well, I'm the perfect test case, pard. Man, I hurt where I don't even have places. There's only one thing makes it the least bit okay."

"What's that?"

Slim Randles - 153

"I keep thinking maybe that sorrel bitch feels as sore and stove up this morning as I do."

"I don't believe I'd count on that."

"Me neither. That stuff ready yet?"

"We'll just take it off the fire and let it steep for a while."

"What's that stuff taste like?"

"Like somebody boiled some green sticks."

"I figured as much."

We sat for a few minutes, then Smokey wrapped a bandana around the rusty can and sipped the hot brew.

"Yee-ikes! Booger that's hot!"

"How's it taste?"

"You say old Indians like this junk?"

"Yep."

"No wonder we ain't got many old Indians anymore," Smokey said, but he tried another sip. In five minutes, he'd drunk nearly all of it.

"Hey, I'm piggin' this. Sorry."

"Drink it all, pard. I'll make some more."

And he did, and we talked some more while the new pot brewed.

"You know," he said, "that stuff's not bad, once you're all through drinkin' it."

"Like beating your head against the wall, huh? Feels so good when you stop."

"That's about right," he said, grinning. "Reminds me of a story this one old boy told us in the bunkhouse . . . that was in Sheridan, Wyoming, I believe. Anyway, this cowboy's originally from down in the Ozarks someplace, you know, where those hillbillies come from? Anyway, he said he went back for Christmas or something one year and he was walking in the country and saw this little kid carrying a dead buzzard in one hand and a twenty-two in the other."

Smokey was smiling now.

"So this cowboy asks the kid, he says what's he going to do with the buzzard and this kid says he's going to eat him. You're kidding, this guy tells the kid. Nope, says the kid. We eat 'em all the time, he says. That about made this cowboy sick, but he looks at the kid and this kid is serious, so he says to the kid, what does buzzard taste like, and this little kid looks right at him and says it tastes 'bout like a owl."

"You lyin' sack . . ."

"Well, that's what he told us."

"'Bout like a owl!"

"I'll go check on the horses," Smokey said, while I laughed and noticed he wasn't limping anymore. He managed to share the next pot of squaw tea with me, and we both got to feeling limber. Of course, the sun was warm, and that must've been the reason.

"By God," Smokey said. "I think those old Paiute ladies know a thing or two."

"Yeah," I said, "I'm feeling pretty perky myself."

"You want to be a cowboy?" Smokey asked.

"What do you mean?"

"Well, you know that a cowboy is a lover, a fighter, and a wild horse rider, right?"

"Oh that. So it's time to be one third of a cowboy, right?"

"I'm going to spur the fur off that old bitch this morning," Smokey said.

"Well, this ain't my favorite third of being a cowboy," I said, "and I know you want to get on that sorrel nightmare real bad, Smoke, but you're going to have to wait your turn."

"How come?"

"Because that mare is going to stomp you into furry pink hog slop, which is okay with me, but I'm going to ride that buckskin first."

"Why?"

"'Cause if you ride first, there won't be anybody here to bury my remains."

He laughed. "Hey! What's this stuff, pard? Ain't we two of the goldamnedest wild horse hunters that ever saddled a horse? Say amen."

"Amen."

"Hallelujah! And has the Good Lord ever made a horse we couldn't handle? Say no."

"No, brother, no!"

"A big amen on that one. And tell me, friend, who is going to step on board that buckskin and make a solid church-going citizen out of that rank lil' sumbuck?"

"I am!"

"I can't hear you, brother."

"I'm going to sit up there tall and straight like I was riding him down to get the mail, and I'll just spur the tallywhacker off that animated sack of dog food!"

"Say amen."

"Amen."

"Let's get saddled up."

We checked the tie ropes on the two broncs and they were good and fast to the corral. Then we took Chuckles and Duster outside the catch pen and tied them to some brush nearby. The mustangs fidgeted some when we led them away, but calmed down when they could see the horses tied outside.

"How do you want to do this?" Smokey asked.

"I've been thinking about this some," I told him. "I'm not getting any younger, and wild horses just don't run over and jump in a guy's lap anymore."

Smokey nodded.

"So I thought, long as I'm feeling about half rank myself, I'd just ride this little booger straight up may the best man win."

Smokey grinned and slapped me on the back.

"Damn! Old Buck's turned into a wolfy son of a BITCH from the high yonders. We're going to ride mustangs. Hide the women and children!"

"Amen," I said, strapping on my chaps. I left my spurs there on the ground. "I think I'll ride him slick-heeled, Smokey. I don't want him getting jabbed if I buck off."

"Buck off? You think you can buck old Buck off?" Smokey started talking quietly to the little buckskin. "You gonna be a quiet little guy and only jump once or twice with old Buck? Now you gotta remember, old Buck here's learned everything he knows about horses by riding them streetcars in the city. So now you gotta be a good little guy and take it easy on him."

I laughed as I dragged the saddle into the pen and laid it by the snubbing post. "Why don't you try sweet talkin' that pretty little sorrel mare of yours and quit botherin' my horse?"

"Hey, pard," Smokey said, rubbing the little mustang's nose, "I pretty near got this little monkey settled down to dog gentle now. Look at this. He likes me."

"You want to ride him, too?"

"No way. He might jump or snort or something, by accident. No, I'm going to have a front-row seat for this one."

Smokey untied the buckskin and turned him gently toward the post in the center of the pen. The little horse took some jerky steps, like he was going to break, but all he did was snort and follow Smokey's soothing voice to the snubbing post.

"See, that wasn't bad," Smokey said, tying him with the old bank robber's hitch.

I took the saddle up to him and waited while he smelled it and jumped back. We went through this for a while, and then I put the saddle down.

"I just figured that I'm not here to gentle this horse," I said. "I think, this once, I'm going to skip all that and just ride this thing."

"Fair and square."

"Code of the West," I said.

"The grandest thing a man can do," Smokey said, grinning.

I slipped my jacket over the buckskin's head for a blind while Smokey held him. Then we got the saddle on and cinched while he hunched up like a big tan inchworm. I talked to him as I took the slack out of the cinch. He boogered a few times, but without being able to see, he wasn't going anywhere. When the cinch was up and snug, I waited a few minutes, then took the rest of the slack up. It would be snug this time, plus it let him get used to the weight on his back.

I did some knee bends and some twisting exercises while Smokey watched and grinned and talked softly to the buckskin.

"How do you feel?" he asked.

"Nervous as a virgin in Alaska," I said.

"Nervous about Little Tommy Tinker here, the kids' pet?"

"I'm just waiting to see you try that sweet little old lady you've got tied there. She keeps looking at you."

"I think she's in love with me," he said. "Must be my rustic charm, what do you think? I think she's got the hots for me."

"I believe she'd like to have you for breakfast, Smoke."

He chuckled. "We'll see who eats what this morning."

With Smokey on the makeshift rope halter I'd fashioned for the horse, I untied the buckskin from the snubbing post, put the lead rope over his neck and tied the other end to the halter, giving me some reins.

You couldn't expect to steer an old pony anywhere much with a rig like that, but at least when I pulled on his head, it wouldn't hurt his mouth.

I took a last hitch in my belts, took the reins and the halter in my left hand, pulled his head around almost to the stirrup, and stepped on.

"You on good?" Smokey whispered.

"Like I was born here, amigo," I said, but I could hear the shaking in my voice. "Best you go dig yourself a hole."

He grinned and scooted over the fence.

Then it was just me and the little buckskin, and I don't know which of us was more scared. He was shaking hard, his muscles bunched up and pushing the cantle of the saddle upward.

"Easy now, son," I said. "We're going to take a little ride together."

Then with my left hand, I released his halter and pulled off the Levi jacket at the same time.

He stood there, blinking at the daylight.

"I told you he was a kid's pet," Smokey said.

Now I swear this. That little horse looked over at Smokey standing there and then his mouth opened, his head dropped, he bellered like a bull in heat, and the seat of that saddle tried to drive me through a cloud.

He took long lunges straight ahead to the fence, then sucked back hard to the left and bellered and jumped. And the thing that all of a sudden shocked me was that I was still on him. I seemed to have both stirrups, and I wasn't even grabbing the horn. That was only because I couldn't find it, friend. Believe me, I was looking. But then something funny came over me. There was a nice crow-hopping rhythm to this tough little stud horse as he bucked around the outer edge of this catch pen, somehow avoiding the sorrel mare at each pass. And with this rhythm came a rhythm from me, and then I realized, by God, this was great!

When he hit the ground, I swung my slick-heeled boots up over his shoulders, contest style, and then swept them back to the cantle when he was airborne. After about four jumps like this, I knew I had him. I took my hat off with my right hand and fanned a bucking horse for the first time ever in my life. Fanned that good wild horse and I gave a yip just out of sheer joy and I could hear Smokey over there screaming like a wounded cat.

"Ride a wild horse!" I heard. "Ride that rank sucker. Whoo-eee!"

And I did.

No one was more surprised than I was when he broke into a trot and went around and around the corral. I took hold of one rope rein and turned his head into the fence then, and he stopped.

"That's a good boy," I said softly. "Good boy."

We both blew hard, then. Real hard. The nervousness had left me, and I was filled with this little secret knowledge that I could ride anything with hair, fly a jet fighter, take out someone's gall bladder, and sing grand opera . . . all the different parts at once. It's never been that way, before or since.

I was glad I hadn't cheated him. And at the same time, I'm glad he didn't cheat me, either.

I reached down and patted his neck and spoke to him until I could feel the muscles relax. Then I took one rein, plowlined him around, and nudged him. He trotted off awkwardly, like a camel, because he wasn't used to carrying the weight, but he trotted with his ears forward and turned several times for me with each rein. I had to stop him by turning him into the fence, but he was all through bucking.

I reached up, pulled his head around to my left stirrup, and stepped down. He stood like a statue while I pulled off the saddle, and I led him to the fence and tied him again.

"Buck," Smokey said, picking up my saddle, "that was a sure-nuf bronc ride. Hey, that was *pretty*."

I was still feeling I could win the Olympic decathlon from a wheelchair. I must have staggered some, but I felt like I was floating.

"I gotta tell you the truth, pard," Smokey said, slapping me on the back, "I thought you'd probably buck off that little horse."

I grinned. "Me, too. Turns out he didn't buck hard like I thought he would."

"I'd hate like hell to see what you think a real bucking horse is," Smokey said. "That one tore it up pretty proud. And if you don't think he bucks hard, just wipe your nose."

I did, and my sleeve came away with blood. It happens that way sometimes when a horse has real power. The force of the bucking can rupture tiny capillaries. I've seen good cowboys bleeding from their noses and even their ears.

We walked out from the corral and sat by the fire pit. I drank the dregs of the green tea cold. It tasted good.

"That was good, Smoke. I don't mind telling you, that was *real* good. At first I was so scared, I didn't know whether I could last even one jump, but then I just got a-goin' on him . . ."

"I know," he said, grinning. "And now, by golly, you're a supreme wild horse rider and ain't it a wonderful life?"

"Amen, brother." I grinned.

"When you get rested up, we'll see if Bessie the Bitch has any spunk in her."

"Hell, I'm ready."

Compared to the sorrel, that little buckskin of mine was a plow horse. I mean, this was *before* Smokey got on. We ended up having to throw and tie this mare before we could get her blindfolded, and then Smokey tied a front foot off the ground with that Montana slip knot I'd heard about. And all this time, that sorrel mare was growling low and evil, like a mountain lion about to strike. With the blindfold in place, she didn't move. She wasn't beaten, but she had to stand still after we got her up. She was standing on just three legs and was blind as a mole. Without sight or footing, no horse is going to move.

I held her head and talked to her, taking care to stand on the near side by the tied-up foot so she couldn't strike me, while Smokey put the saddle on her.

"She's bloating on me," Smokey said. "I think I'll let her move a little first, just to be safe."

He cinched up, then told me to run for it. He snatched off the blindfold and hopped behind the snubbing post.

Well, she didn't attack or anything, but she did fight and sling her head and buck the best she could on three legs while being tied to the snubbin' post. We only needed her to jump around a little so she'd let out her air and Smokey could cinch her up.

"I just thought of something, Buck," Smokey yelled through the growing plume of dust near the snubbin' post.

"What's that?"

"How we gonna get the blind back on her without getting killed?"

It was something to ponder, all right. I guess we could've gotten the ropes on her and thrown her again, but I was in just that kind of a euphoric trance that all of a sudden everything just looked so easy and simple. I walked over, stepped to one side as she bit at me, and jumped on her head. We both went down, but I was on top. She was screaming now, and her teeth clacked together as she looked for me, but I was unshakable today. I could move mountains; I could swim rivers. Refer to taking out gall bladders a little while back there for the rest of the list.

"You're a crazy man!" Smokey yelled.

I looked up at him from the thrashing horse.

"You gonna stand there all day visiting, or are you gonna blindfold this bitch?"

He got the blinds on and me off, and the sorrel mare lurched to her feet. Smokey took the cinch up good and snug before she could bloat up on him again.

"If I didn't know any better," I said, "I'd say that was a wild horse."

"Looks like one," Smokey said, doing deep knee bends.

"Can't be," I said. "She's wearing a Slash G brand on her shoulder. Probably some old lady's Sunday afternoon horse that wandered away from the barn."

"You show me that old lady," he said, "and I'll pay her entry fees." He grinned. "And you know you can go to hell for lyin', too."

And then I looked at Smokey and the grin that came from his face was different, somehow, than it had been. And then I realized that his smile before had a certain forced quality to it, while this one now came freely and easily. This grin knocked about twenty years off him, and if you erased some of the map marks from around his eyes, and did a dye job on the curly hair, he could have passed for someone that high school girls' mothers warned them about.

"She's gonna be wicked," I said, seriously. He didn't blink.

"Probably," he said.

"You don't have to do this, you know."

"Now what the hell do you mean by that?"

"Look, Smokey, in your condition . . . well, riding a bucking horse can't help you any."

And he stood there looking at me and the grin stayed just as big on his face and he said quietly, "You mean I might die, or something like that?"

I didn't know what to say, so I just grinned, too.

"Showtime," Smokey said, fixing his reins and pulling her head around. Leaving the blindfold on, and without releasing her head, he pulled the foot rope to let the near front hoof down. She was shaking like a powder keg on a waterbed, her muscles clenching and unclenching. Smokey sat back in the saddle and swung his spurs up ahead of the cinch and smiled at me.

"Hail Mary and all that stuff," he said and jerked off the blind. That sorrel mare slammed him back in the saddle on the first jump, then came leaping and twisting straight for me. Until that moment I had forgotten that I was standing there like a bowlegged target and suddenly recalled my recent decathlon prowess and managed to clear that six-foot fence without touching it.

That rank mama was screaming now with frustration and her bucking got wilder. She jumped higher off the ground than before and shook while she was up there, but while this kind of bucking looks spectacular to a rodeo audience, it really isn't that difficult to handle.

Smokey was riding well, sweeping spurs back and forth with that soft, buzzing sound.

And then it was as if they were dancing, the two of them. Through the dust, the bucking seemed to lose some of its hard edge, and it was kind of beautiful, the two of them dodging and dancing together around the catch pen.

She'd seem to be wearing out and she'd slow down a little, and just when I thought she'd break from the bucking and quit, she just grunted and threw it all at Smokey.

And my pard was very busy and very serious, but he was enjoying it. He was doing it well. This was grand stuff, out here with only me and the horses to see. It was the ride of his life, and he had never put more into it.

The bucking had been long and noisy and serious, so when the sorrel quit, it startled us. There was no tapering off into little crow-hops. She went up for a pile-driving high dive, and when she came down she just stood there in her tracks while the dust around her settled.

Smokey fanned her with his hat, but she just stood there with her ears back and hated. He tried to untrack her with first one rein, then the other, to get her moving, but she just rubber-necked around and wouldn't move.

Finally, Smokey cheeked her around and stepped off. She didn't offer to bite or strike, so he took the saddle off and tied the end of the lead rope to the snubbin' post.

"What a ride, Smoker!" I said. "I've never seen anything like it. That would've been first money anywhere."

"Thanks," he said, but he kept looking at that mare. Her eyes never left him, and her ears were laid back.

"You see how she quit like that?"

"It was *right now*, wasn't it?"

"Would you trust that mare to be broke?"

"Now that you mention it . . ."

"I wouldn't trust that sweetie to eat breakfast. She's got a bad attitude, and I think she's decided to wait for her chance."

I didn't know what to say, but it didn't matter. Before I could say anything, we both heard the helicopter.

Chapter Nineteen

THE BIG, ROARING MACHINE WITH NAVY MARKINGS sat down nearby in a nest of swirling dust. A very tall man waved to the pilot, hunched over, and trotted until he cleared the blades, then walked over to us at the corral.

"You boys got any makin's?" he asked.

"Yes, sir," Smokey said, digging out his sack of Bull Durham. The helicopter pilot kept the thing idling in the background, but the dust was no longer pelting us.

This man was wearing civilian clothes, was tall and angular, and his face and hands were leathered like an old saddle. He had the look about him, and it surprised us to see it on a man who just got out of a military machine.

He rolled and lit one and then dropped into a hunker. So did we.

"Kinda far from home, aren't you?"

"Yes, sir."

"Don't suppose you know where you are, right?" he asked.

"In the middle of the China Lake Naval Weapons Center," I said.

"Wrong," he said. "You see, you boys have got the wrong answers already. Now if you fellas were in the middle of the bombing range, I'd have to report it, and there'd come more of these choppers filled with nineteen-year-old kids with rifles. You boys ever notice how serious a nineteen-year-old kid with a rifle is? They don't seem to have imagination anymore. Too bad, too. See, they'd think anybody riding around up here was some goddammed spy or something and would arrest them, confiscate their horses, take them in and question the bejeesus out of them for about three days, and then turn them loose. Now that doesn't sound like fun, does it?"

"No, sir," we both said.

"Personally, I can find better ways to spend my time, too," he said.

He took another drag on the quirlie and looked at both of us.

"You think that sorrel can be trusted?" he asked.

"What?"

"The sorrel. Horse quits like that, I'd just as leave shoot it for dog food, don't you think?"

"You saw Smokey ride that mare?" I asked.

"Hell, boys, you was raising so much dust we thought old Coso Peak was going to blow its top again. That's why we came out here. Damn nice ride, by the way."

"Much obliged," Smokey grinned.

"Now the way I see it, you boys were just concerned about the well-being of the government's horses, isn't that about right?"

"I don't understand," I said.

"Well, what else would you be doing riding one of the government's own personal mustangs?" he said. "Look at it for a minute. Everybody, including you, knows that it's been illegal to catch and sell wild horses for years now."

"Yes, sir."

"So it can't be that was what you were doing, obviously. Any damn fool can see what happened. You saw these two horses, noticed how out of shape they were, and wanted to help them by exercising them. That law don't say a thing against physical fitness. Am I right?"

"I believe that's right, sir." Smokey was grinning now.

"Now, as for where you decided to exercise these mustangs. I know you boys don't know this, or you'd be in trouble, but this mountain range is off limits to anybody but Navy types and a few crusty old civilian desert rats they hire to keep an eye on the range conditions. Do you understand?"

"Yes, sir."

"Way I figure it, you boys was out for a nice afternoon ride someplace when suddenly you were caught up in one of those dense ground fogs that London and the Mojave Desert are so famous for. Isn't that about what happened?"

"Yes, sir," Smokey said, grinning. "We was goin' fishing."

The lanky man grinned straight down at the ground and his eyes twinkled as he studied us.

"There," he said. "You see how far lost a guy can get when that fog moves in?"

"It's treacherous, sir," I said. I was beginning to think I wouldn't spend the rest of my life in a government rest camp near Leavenworth, Kansas.

"Now I realize the visibility is pretty bad today," he said, looking for miles across desert mountain ranges. "That's why I couldn't find what was causing that dust and that's why this conversation never took place and you've never seen me before, right?"

We nodded.

"But tomorrow is supposed to be clear weather, and I'll have to fly out here and investigate the dust cloud. It wouldn't be a real good idea for anybody to be in this mountain range tomorrow, would it?"

"No, sir."

"Now if those two horses were running around out here tomorrow, a person couldn't say they'd been stolen from the government, could he?"

"No, sir."

He stood up, started to leave, then turned back to us.

"Boys," he said, "the Navy's getting ready to build some things in this part of the range that it doesn't want you or me to know anything about. You've probably heard how fussy they can get about these things."

We nodded.

"Well," he said, "they'll be all over this area from now on. The mustangin' here is all done. This is it. You might try Nevada, maybe. Or Wyoming."

"Sir," said Smokey, "would you happen to have a camera with you?"

"I believe I do."

"Could I take a picture with it?"

"It's one of those instant things," he said.

"That's perfect," my partner said.

The man went to the helicopter and returned with the camera. Smokey asked if he would get a picture of the sorrel mare for him.

"You want that fresh brand to show, or not?" he asked.

"I'd like that in the picture," Smokey said.

So he went in the corral and got a sideways shot of that mare, and it came out okay, and the man handed it to Smokey.

"About time to open that gate, isn't it?" he asked.

We took the makeshift halters off both mustangs, opened the gate, and saw them run up the ridge and out of sight.

"I'll be leaving now," the man said. "You might think about doing the same."

"Yes, sir," I said. "Mind if I ask a question? You haven't even asked us for identification or anything."

He just grinned.

"Boys, no Russian spy ever born would be stupid enough to ride a bronc."

He clapped Smokey on the shoulder and started away, then turned back to look at us. "And he wouldn't be able to ride it that well, either."

Then he was gone, the noise of his helicopter clattering off down the canyon until it was quiet again, and we were left with Chuckles and Duster and our own thoughts.

"I think that was a compliment, there at the end," Smokey said.

"That's my pard," I said. "Razor sharp, as usual. I think we'd better saddle up and go home."

Smokey picked up his saddle and headed for Duster.

"Only one thing bothers me, Kemosabi," he said.

"What's that?"

"Just who *was* that masked man?"

Chapter Twenty

WE DIDN'T EAT ANYTHING AT ALL until we had both horses loaded in the truck and were heading north again toward dry Owens Lake. The sun was behind the peaks to the west now and it would be dark soon. There were lights way far off there at a ranch or a mine.

We grabbed what we could from the grub sack and ate until we thought we might live out the day.

"You ever been dirtier?" Smokey asked, after a long silence.

"I don't think so."

"Want to stop at Dirty Sock and soak in the pool?"

"To be honest, right now I just want to get these horses home and lie down on something and sleep for maybe a week or year or something like that."

"Then how about a cup of coffee in Lone Pine?"

"You're on."

Darkness slid in on us when we were circling Owens Lake, and it was beautiful.

"I'm sorry it turned out the way it did," I told Smokey. "I know you wanted to sell some horses."

"Sell horses?" he said. "You crazy or something?"

I just looked at him.

"See?" he said. "That's the trouble with cowboys. No common sense. First of all, Buck, it's been illegal to catch wild horses for what, seven years?"

I grinned.

"And then if you did catch them and break them and haul them to town, ain't worth nothing right now. Wouldn't be worth a man's time to mess with them. And a guy'd have to wake up and find himself sleeping alone in a sandstorm somewhere, and he'd have to learn to like cheeseburgers at the Pines Café. You know the Pines Café, don't you? That's the place where they don't put any tablecloths on the tables."

I was laughing pretty good now.

"And tell me, Oh Wise One," I said. "What do you recommend for a happy life?"

"I'm glad you asked, my dear fellow," Smokey said. "It is simply a matter of doing the civilized thing. That is what makes you happy."

"And what, pray tell, is the civilized thing?"

"Why, it's living in a city with thick brown air, and driving a car and honking your horn at some dumb dude who isn't going fast enough. Are you hearing this?"

"Clearly, Oh Most Wise."

"Please take notes. There's one of them quizzes later, you see. So now that you're in the city and are mad enough at everyone else, the next thing to do is find a job that you hate. That's very important. In the city, you have to earn a lot of money to get by. To earn a lot of money, you have to take a job you can't stand."

"Why's that?"

"Why, that's so simple everybody knows it, you ignorant wild horse hunter. The awfuller a job is, the more money they pay you for it. Did you know garbagemen make more money than schoolteachers? It's a fact. That's because nobody wants to be a garbageman.

"Now let me ask you a question, cowboy," Smokey said. "All the smart people who go to college make more money than the dumb ones, right?"

"I guess."

"Wrong again, Buckaroo," he said, grinning. "As a matter of fact, the dumb ones make all the money."

"How you figure that?"

"It's easy. You tell me this: is it smarter to work at a job you love, or a job you hate?"

"It's definitely smarter to work at a job you love," I said, grinning.

"Then the dumb people got all the jobs they hate, which pay a lot of money, and that's what's wrong with the world today."

"What?"

"You see, women all want to marry dumb guys who make a lot of money. They have babies with these guys, which then makes the babies at least half dumb, am I right?"

"Right."

"So what happens to the smart guys of this world? Those poor bastards are out there in the open air, singing like larks and coursing like eagles . . ."

"Coursing like eagles?"

"'Course they are! Hey, I read *Popular Mechanics* . . ."

"You lie like a rug, too."

"So there are the smart guys, coursing like eagles over dale and vale and hump and bump . . ."

"Cheerful in their demeanor . . ."

"Yes, but horny as old goats because no smart woman wants to marry a happy man and give him smart kids. So what happens? The half-dumb babies from the city marry other half-dumb babies from the city, and the bloodlines of the world just go plumb to hell. Them dumb ones just keep marrying dumber and dumber in the city and the first thing you know, they're all inbred and scrubby."

"So tell me, Professor Smoke, what is your solution to this dilemma?"

"There's two solutions, really. One is to castrate all the dumb guys making all the money, and the other is to pay us smart guys more to be happy."

"You might have trouble getting solution number one through Congress," I said, "but number two has real possibilities."

"Stop the truck!" Smokey yelled.

I braked quickly and pulled over as the last high sunlight of a late spring day turned the snow pink on the 14,000-foot peaks. Smokey walked out away from the truck.

"Come with me," he said.

I followed along until we stood well clear of the truck and were looking across the darkened valley toward the big mysterious mountains to the west.

"Now you will repeat after me," Smokey said, cupping his hands to his mouth. "I am a smart man!"

"I am a smart man!"

"Women can't stand me!"

"Speak for yourself," I told him.

"I am," he said.

"Women can't stand me, either!" I yelled.

"That's much better," he said, quietly. "It's great to be alive!"

"It's great to be alive!"

"I'm a wild horse ridin' sumbitch from the tall rocks!"

"And, by God, so am I!" I yelled. Then we both laughed.

"I won't go live in the city anymore!" he yelled.

I stood there for a minute. Somehow I knew this was coming, and I knew the time called for a commitment. It seemed like a snap decision, on the face of it, but we both knew this had been working slowly around for a month now. Or maybe more. Maybe it started coming at those parties where it was against the rules to laugh. Or maybe on the freeways, or every time I reached for the bottle of little pills at work. There were things to consider. On one hand was the good job. On the other were a lot of things. The way my muscles felt right then, the music of the mountains, the way the desert looks when it's waking up. But all there really needed to be on that side of the scale was the way I'd felt that morning wiping the blood from my dust-coated face. It wasn't much of a contest.

"Do it," Smokey said.

"I won't go live in the city anymore!" I yelled.

We laughed and got back in the truck, and the horses didn't think we were crazy, or if they did, they didn't care, and we drove along in the comforting blackness toward hot coffee.

"You know," Smokey said, "that was a damfool thing to do, Buck."

"What was that?"

"Give up a good job to go off and play cowboy."

"Pardner," I told him, "it's about the grandest thing a man can do."

"Amen."

Chapter Twenty-One

THE ENVELOPE HAD COME while we were away in the Cosos. In fact, it had come several weeks ago. There was no note, just a key to a storage locker and an address.

"Need to use the phone?" Ross asked.

I just shook my head and walked the four blocks from the ranch at the edge of town to the phone booth by the Standard station. I loaded up with change and made the call.

Jan was past the answering machine stage by this time. Yes, the children missed me and asked about me. Yes, she missed me sometimes, too. No, she didn't think that would be a good idea. It was a lot simpler, didn't I see, that we just broke clean now before we got hurt. But I was really hurt now. We didn't know each other, though, did we? And it was just better this way. Well, let's give it some time and think about it a bit and maybe then we can see each other. She wasn't closing the door completely, but there would have to be some changes, some ground rules. No, she was certain she and the kids couldn't live in the country. She wouldn't know what to do and there was school and their friends and her job and all, but hey, it was nice to hear my voice and why didn't we write each other a bit and see if that would help things? Let's not talk about divorce because maybe after a while we could find a way to make things work. What was I going to do for work? Oh, she saw, and would that be enough for me? What about writing? Maybe a little of that, too. Well, that was good at least, because she thought I had a talent that way, you know. And, yes, she realized how strongly I felt about my friend, and could understand strong friendships like that, but she still didn't understand it all, but would be thinking about it.

In the meantime, I should write her. And write the kids. They really did love me, you know. And let's just write instead of call for a while and think about things and who knows?

I took the next hour to walk around the town. Independence was getting ready for the onset of fishing season. Red Austin was unpacking boxes of fishing lures for his stores, O.K. Kelley's gas station was making room for more quarts of oil in the window, and the motels were repairing their neon vacancy signs, which seemed to go on the blink each winter. The locust trees and cottonwoods had their new spring "pinfeather" leaves of that delicate, fresh light green, and the little town just smelled cleaner than it does later when the hordes of Los Angeles fishermen pour through it on their ways to the higher, cooler country to the north.

So there is still a chance. That's good. I'm going to try for that chance. I'm going to write those letters, too. But she'll have to bend a little, as well. It wasn't good, living in her house like that. Maybe if we live in a house I provide, things will straighten out. And maybe if we live up here on my own turf, things will be better. The kids would love it.

It'll be a second courting, and it may not work, but I have time to try, and I will. Hope? Oh yes. She's a good woman. But she married a cowboy, God help us both. I know that now. I can't be a writer who rides horses. It can't work that way. I have to be a cowboy who writes, and I just pray that will be good enough for Jan someday.

I just shook my head and walked back to the ranch. It was a bone-weary day, when the strenuous day I spent yesterday, coupled with long hours, made everything move in slow motion.

I heard the phone call again, every word, and yet the weariness gave it the soft-focus patina of an Impressionist painting. What was left was the feeling of the conversation. What was left was the feeling of the wild horse hunt. What was left was the mood of a little town getting ready for summer.

Anymore bad news, world? Let's have it now when my mind and body are numbed. Heap it on. Don't hold anything back. Do your damndest. I'll learn to worry about each of them tomorrow, but today I'll just walk among the tall locust trees and enjoy the soft spring sun and remember how it felt to ride that buckskin. Was that only yesterday?

The weariness blurred events together some, too. It was hard to trust memory, because memory was just sitting there in idle, enjoying the sunshine, too.

That morning, after our dose of eggs fried in pepper, Smokey took the truck to Lone Pine, but not before he gave the photograph of that sorrel mare to old Grant.

"That's her," he said, his face lighting up. "By God, you boys did it! Ross, look at this and you tell me if that isn't that sorrel mare."

"Sure looks like her, Grant," Ross smiled.

"Take a look at her shoulder, Grant," Smokey said.

The old man moved up to where the lamp shone directly on the photo.

"That there looks like a Slash G," he said, quietly.

"That *is* a Slash G, Grant," Smokey said. "We couldn't bring her home, but she's your mare forever now."

The old man sat back down very quietly and just kept looking at the photo with his good eye. Ross grinned at us and nodded. We had done all right.

"Hell, goddang I mean to say, the way it was, now you take in there that sorrel mare there," Grant said quietly. "She give you boys much trouble?"

I started to speak and Smokey nudged me.

"Grant, that mare of yours is the rankest old bitch that ever lived."

"You don't say!"

"Ain't that right, Buck?" I nodded. "It's a pure-t fact that old heifer like to bit old Buck's britches off, and she did a tap dance on my belly twice."

The old timer grinned and shook his head.

"Hell," Smokey said. "It took all both of us could do to get her saddled and blindfolded, but we couldn't get her rode. You might have been able to ride her when you were a bit younger, Grant, but we sure couldn't. I bet there ain't ten men in the country who could get that one straightened out."

"That's the truth," I said. I was glad I finally had something true that I could agree with.

"She's a dandy, ain't she boys?"

"One in a million," Smokey said.

I walked through the ranch yard, folding up bailing wire and chucking it into some rusty drums over by the shop. What a morning. Too many things to think about. But I knew one thing. I had a ton of regrets for this last month, but I'd do it again.

Ross and I ate a quiet lunch together, as Smokey was still down in Lone Pine, and Grant went to the Pines Café with his photograph.

"Things kinda tough right now?" Ross asked.

"No," I said. "No, I don't think so. Things are all right."

"You going back down?" he asked later on over coffee.

"Maybe a little later."

Ross didn't say anything.

"I been thinking," I said.

"That sounds dangerous," Ross chuckled.

"Ross, you still have that cabin up in the Inyos?"

"It's still there."

"I was thinking maybe, if you needed some colts ridden, that I might hole up there for a while. That is, if it's okay with you if I stay up there."

"Hell, I don't care," he said. "There's some young stuff out in pasture I guess you could fool with. Tell you the truth, I could use a little help with the gather, first."

I nodded. "Sure."

"That's a lonely place up there," Ross said.

"That's okay," I said. "I think that will suit me just fine."

"I'll come up every month or two and see if you've gone crazy on us yet."

"I'll have the coffee on," I said, smiling.

Smokey didn't get back until after supper that evening, and we were both so tired, we didn't even talk until the next morning.

Smokey was smiling then, and I was feeling better. I'd straightened out Ross's tack room a bit for him just because I needed something to do. I was just finishing when Smokey came in.

"Look, look, look, said Jane. See the editor get all dirty. Naughty, naughty, naughty!"

"You go to hell," I said, laughing.

"Ross tells me you're staying on," he said. "Guess things didn't work out at home, huh?"

"Doesn't look good right now, but to tell you the truth, I just don't know. I called my boss this morning and told him I was quitting the bright lights for something better."

"You tell him what that something better was?"

I laughed. "Yep. 'Fraid so."

"And he ordered an immediate psychiatric examination?"

"He'd have to find me first," I said. "And where'd you learn big words like that? You been reading cereal boxes again?"

"I ask the waitresses for help with the longer ones."

"How about you, Smoke? Back to Wyoming?"

"I don't think so," he said. "A long time now, I been thinking about Utah."

"Utah? What'd you lose in Utah?"

"Nothing, really," he said. "But I've been over there and looked around. You ever seen that canyon country they got? Wildest damn place you ever been. Buck, I've looked down in them red ol' smooth-rocked canyons and there's this little trickle of water down in the bottoms of them, and sometimes a few cottonwood trees and enough grass for a horse or two."

"You got a job lined up?"

"No. Oh, I'll get a job sooner or later, of course, but I've got a little put by and I'm just going to find me the deepest, nastiest canyon I can find—one with no Jeep tracks anywhere near it—and I'm going to build a stone cabin in the darkest corner of that monster I can find. I don't want to hear anything but birds and lizards and maybe a horse."

"Sounds like a lot of work to me," I said, slapping the tack room dust off me and moving out into the sunlight. "You sure you're up to that kind of labor, amigo?"

"And why the hell *wouldn't* I be?"

"Well, your . . . problem, Smoke. I mean, how long will you be able to get around and do things?"

"Oh hey," he said, "did I forget to tell you?"

"Tell me what?"

"About that cancer stuff," he said. "You see, I was up there running wild horses and eating your cooking and living a clean life and damned if I didn't start feeling better. Now, when I got back here I says to myself, 'Self,' I said, 'isn't it strange to feel better?' And I allowed as how it probably was. So yesterday in Lone Pine, while I was shopping, I just nipped in to the old hospital there and the doctor said it was a miracle, but mustangin' cured my cancer."

"What?"

"Cleared that sumbitch up just like nothing," he said, grinning.

I dropped the broom.

"You!" I yelled as it sank in. "You! You faked it? You dirty bastard, you *faked* it?"

He grinned and backed out of the tack room into the yard.

"Now Buck." He grinned. "You know the old saying, that there's something about the outside of a horse that's good for the inside of a man."

"You never did have anything wrong with you!"

"Well, my left arm gets pains in it about every two weeks . . ."

"You bastard!"

I didn't know whether to laugh, cry, or kill him. "You lousy bastard! All this time I think you're dying and you're faking it. Sonofabitch!"

"Sticks and stones can break my bones," he said, grinning and backing away from me.

"Before I end your sick little miserable life," I said, "I want to know why."

"Now you wouldn't hit an old mustangin' pard like me, would you?"

"Why?" I said. "Why did you do that?"

He just shrugged his shoulders, grinned wider, and kept backing away toward the haystack.

"Why put me through all that crap about you having cancer and dying? Why? You bastard, tell me why?"

"You were getting soft down there, Buck," he said.

"So?"

"So what would I have to say to get you out of there for a while?"

I thought about it for a minute.

"You would've come if I said I needed a vacation?"

"No."

I was torn between emotions leading me to either hug him or tear out his throat.

"Damn it, Smoke! I mean, that's not something you put a guy through because you think he needs some exercise!"

"And if he needs a new life?"

By this time, I'd backed him up to the haystack. I picked up a pitchfork, murmured an appropriate expletive, and stabbed it deep into the hay. Then I sat down on a bale and just looked at Smokey. He sat down, too, once he decided his life wasn't in danger, and we just sat there looking at each other until I quit shaking my head and started grinning. He gave me a light punch in the arm and grinned more, and then we were both laughing. Laughing, like two of God's worst feeble-minded monkeys under a spring sky with the breeze going through the locust trees. I knew then that we weren't too old for anything. We were still two boys who thought they were rank enough to ride anything with hair and whip anything with an attitude.

"So you just decided to play God and rearrange everyone's lives for them, huh?"

He nodded his head and kept laughing.

"You could've been a great television preacher," I told him, "or a used-car salesman."

"Never would make a good carpenter, though," he said.

"Not unless you could do it horseback."

"I wouldn't have been much as a surgeon, either," he said. "What do you think?"

"Well, if all they needed was to field dress someone . . ."

"Yeah, I could handle that all right."

"I had a dude over Sawmill Pass once," I said, "was a doctor. This guy, with all his education, couldn't start a fire to save his butt. He dragged in a green log and held a match to it and wondered why it didn't burn. Well, I was about sixteen or seventeen then, and I remember thinking how dumb this guy was because he couldn't start a fire. And one day, a few days later, I was thinking to myself that I might look pretty dumb trying to take someone's appendix out, too."

Smokey nodded, then walked away from the haystack to the shade of the locusts by the stained wooden shop to roll a smoke. I followed him over.

"You crazy bastard," I said softly. "You just decided I needed saving?"

He grinned. "You glad you came?"

"Yes," I answered, honestly.

"No regrets?"

"Of course I have regrets, Smoke! Dammit! It's . . . aw hell, I don't know."

"Then I guess it all worked out okay, didn't it?"

I just smiled.

"But a whole wild horse hunt? You left a job for a wild horse hunt?"

"But wasn't it a *dandy* wild horse hunt?"

"Yes it was, amigo. It was a pip. But I still don't understand . . ."

Smokey looked straight at me. "Let's just say I owed one to Crystal's Uncle Buck."

The next day, Smokey threw his war bag and bedroll and saddle on a Greyhound bus and went off to find his canyon. I offered to drive him over there and help him build the place, but he said he wanted to do it by himself, just the way he wanted it, and he'd let me know when it was done and I could come over and stay for a while.

"But where can I get hold of you?" I asked.

"Oh," he said, shaking my hand, "don't worry about it, city boy. I'll find you. Always have."

"Yep. You always have."

"Keep a leg on each side and your mind in the middle, pard."

"You too," I said as he got on and went down the road again. Just as he always did.

Chapter Twenty-Two

Dogs around the sun
Cats around the moon
I'll ride that pony
'long about June.

I WORKED THE GATHER WITH ROSS that spring, then ended up packing mules most of the summer. I wrote a lot of letters to Jan, too, and I discovered I was really getting to like her. In the fall, I took a few days off to go deer hunting, and then I took a handful of junior candidates for horsedom and brought them up here to this little board cabin by the spring in the high Inyos.

The little guys and I just took our time with it, playing around with one another, learning and getting the boogers and then getting over the boogers and all of that. Before long, they could carry me around these rough old mountains and have as much fun at it as I did.

Sometimes I'd get in the mood for a cheeseburger at the Pines, or a hot shower, and I'd drive on down the canyon to the ranch and have a little friendly palaver with Ross and Grant. But mostly, my life was up in those piñons at the cabin with those young horses.

It became a somewhat settled life for me. It became very comfortable.

To tell you the truth, I hardly ever thought about Smokey those days. He was responsible for this, of course, and when I got bucked off in a rock pile, I felt quite free to use his name in vain. And there were times when the mountains were just right and the music came and that little dry breeze came whispering up, and at those times, I'd kind of grin and nod my head in the general direction of Utah. But most of the time, I just figured old Smoke would let me know when he got his place done, or maybe he was in Mexico chasing skirts, or maybe he'd show up here in camp some night, broke and needing a meal.

My life settled into a routine, but it's a routine I savor. The pre-dawn news on the radio while the coffee and the cabin are warming up. The morning inspection of each of my youngsters out there in the corral, checking shoes, touching them all over, spending the time to talk to them while they eat. Savoring the riding, and later the exploring of the Inyo Mountains as each of them learns. I had decided that these little horses were going to be the gentlest, most reliable mountain horses anyone ever put a small child on. When one would reach that point, I'd take him down the hill to the ranch and pick up another young knothead ready for kindergarten. And I'd get the mail.

And in the mountain evenings up at the little cabin, I pick one colt who is teetering on the cusp of trustworthy and ride him up the trail that switchbacks from the spring to the top of the ridge, and we just sit there. Sometimes the winds are raking clouds out of the Sierra peaks across the darkening Owens Valley, and they come to us on the ridge and make us cold. Sometimes it's just one of those quiet times, looking down at that tiny cluster of man-stars on the black valley floor that is Independence. Oh, it still looks the same as it did twenty years ago, even if I don't anymore.

This view from the ridge gives you an interesting perspective, too. From up here it always seems as though the people recoiled from the sheer mass of the mountains that hemmed them in and huddled together for comfort. Maybe that isn't too far wrong, at that.

Perhaps my daily visit to this overlook about a mile straight up from those lights is just to reassure myself that life and electricity go on somewhere in the world. Or maybe it's just a pleasant new habit with no serious purpose. After all, part of the charm of sharing a cabin with nothing but memories is the acquisition of frivolous habits. Doing a certain thing in a certain manner at a certain time of day without the danger of offending or interfering with someone else is a partial salve for the quiet ache of sleeping alone. I'll have to include that in the next letter to Jan. She seems to enjoy them.

I'll keep working on that, with everything I have. The dark-haired girl still comes, most of the time. But lately, the last few early mornings, I look at the dark-haired girl and she smiles and it's Jan's smile. The same smile she gave me that last morning, and I can't help it and I don't know what it means.

But up on this ridge in the evenings, the intangible broom in the soft desert night breeze sweeps away the petty aches and problems and gives a man a chance to think of things greater than himself... or at least gives him the opportunity to think of something. And there are also those times when it is just too pretty to think.

I guess that's why, when the letter arrived from Bishop, I wasn't ready for it.

Dear Buck,

I thought you'd like to know Smokey passed away last month. You know he was sick for a long time.

He was living here at the last in a little apartment near us, and Crystal went over and straightened for him sometimes when he got to where he couldn't do it for himself. The sherrif used to check on him, and he was who found him. He passed away in his chair.

By the way, Wilson and me taken care of the arangements at the funeral home, for Crystal's sake, so there is nothing to do.

I know you were good friends, so I thought you should know.

Your friend,
Claudia (Kitten)

I got old Duster up out of the pasture that trip, put shoes on him, and hauled him up here to help me with this new batch of babies. He makes a great snubbing horse for a fractious youngster and quiets them down. There's something soothing to a colt about having an older horse there letting him know there's really nothing to get excited about.

And sometimes, when it seems the south wind can bring the sound of mustangs' hooves clear up this canyon from those wild Cosos down there below the dry lake, sometimes then I'll saddle up this sabino my pard once caught a wild horse with, and I'll ride him up here for a look at the world.

There are questions to ask, of course. Questions about the past and about the future. So many questions it hurts to try them all out. So we just dump all that and ride up here. And we can look south to that mottled tangle of rocks called the Cosos and watch them shimmer a bit from the mirage waves above Owens Lake and we can think of wild horses and friends.

Then I reach down and pat my partner's horse on the neck and say, "I know, boy. Me too."

060538